CROSSRO
LOVE UNDERCOVER

Dixie Lynn Dwyer

MENAGE EVERLASTING

Siren Publishing, Inc.
www.SirenPublishing.com

A SIREN PUBLISHING BOOK
IMPRINT: Ménage Everlasting

CROSSROADS 6: LOVE UNDERCOVER
Copyright © 2016 by Dixie Lynn Dwyer

ISBN: 978-1-68295-792-9

First Printing: November 2016

Cover design by Les Byerley
All art and logo copyright © 2016 by Siren Publishing, Inc.

Printed in the U.S.A.

PUBLISHER
Siren Publishing, Inc.
www.SirenPublishing.com

CROSSROADS 6: LOVE UNDERCOVER

DIXIE LYNN DWYER
Copyright © 2016

Prologue

"This situation just keeps getting worse and worse. First, our contact is a no-show, and now we're in the middle of a fucking dessert city and the location has changed on our terrorist cell. I don't like this. Shit is getting screwed up," Spence, Sacha Smith's team leader, stated aloud while he was going over information from informants.

"Listen you're the one that said this operation was a sure thing. That all our ducks are in a row and we have six other agents in that fucking building right now. If you think this is a set-up and that your informants are working for Black Out, then we need to pull this operation now. Otherwise, I'm heading in to do my part. I will help Charro get the evidence we need from that office. You need to handle the other shit," Sacha said as she gave him a firm expression.

"We need as much evidence as we can get, or else we've got nothing, and if we get caught, these men loyal to Black Out will torture and kill us."

"I know."

He stood up and placed his hand on her shoulder. "You shouldn't be the one to be doing this. It's not even your job."

She raised her hand up. "I was trained for this, and it's not like I'm not experienced."

"But these men are different, Sacha. You can't let them capture you. The things they've done to people, to women and children who stood in the way of their cause."

"I don't plan on getting captured."

He let his hand fall and exhaled. "Anya should have been here by now. It's becoming clear that she didn't make it. You realize that, don't you?"

"Yes, and it makes it even more important and crucial that I go in there. These men, the ones who are part of this terrorist cell, need to be identified. We need specific faces of the masterminds behind this. Not just their front men. This is our last chance, or the mission is a wash. We head home, and these people get away with succeeding in whatever it is they have planned. I can do this. Plus, Charro has the more difficult job. He has to get into that building and get to that safe and find those documents."

"Be safe, Sacha, and when this is over, you and I need a sit-down. Just the two of us."

Her belly tightened, and she saw that expression in his eyes. He liked her. He wanted them to be more than just co-agents, friends, but there was just something about him that didn't make her see him in that way at all. Plus, he seemed kind of weak in some ways, and she wasn't even certain how he'd gained this position with the agency, but it wasn't her problem. She'd worked her way through having to prove herself to way tougher men and leaders than Spence. She just wanted back into the United States where she would feel a lot safer and could move on to the next case.

That made her think about Charro. Now him she could see herself falling into bed with. But not now while partners on a mission. Maybe when all was done, and things were normal, she could let him know she could spend part of her time off with him. The thought both scared her and frightened her. She did alone better. Once there was a connection, a bond with people, leaving them became a heartache and losing them was part of being a soldier. Mates just didn't stick around between missions. She's seen it hundreds of times.

This situation was supposed to have been resolved weeks ago. She was ready to go home. She didn't feel confident about the last twelve hours of this operation at all. But she had to see it through. It was her job, and she would make sure she did a hundred percent, no matter what.

It was times like this that she wished there were someone in charge who had guts and more experience. Spence had been a desk guy for most of his career. Sacha had been in the middle of the heat since she'd entered the Marine Corps at twenty. She'd followed her father and brother Franco's footsteps, and not a day had gone by that she regretted it. She loved her country, and she had talents and abilities that became assets to this special unit she belonged to.

Certain missions appealed to her or, rather, honed in on her patriotic side. This terrorist cell, Black Out, was one of many. What made them key to stop was their ability to remain hidden and undetected and the chatter from reliable sources that claimed Black Out was going to strike a series of locations in terrorist acts that would kill innocent women and children.

There was some chatter in the last several hours that indicated information on thumb drives or other evidence proving who these men were. They had nothing but false identities thus far, and she was still not certain that these men were from Kabul. Something told her they were from somewhere else.

It was believed that the thumb drives and microchips contained maps, times, locations, and the names of people involved with the group. It was a copy, made by an undercover operative who'd planted the materials in this safe. The problem was that they weren't the only ones looking for these copies. Members of Black Out were, too, and they were closing in. So much so that several other soldiers in her team needed to be placed in strategic positions to intervene while

Charro got to the room and the safe. The sons of bitches were closer than they realized, and because they'd waited so long, they would all be risking their lives for these thumb drives and chips. Charro was furious, and so was Sacha.

But she had his back. She knew this was a last chance. She would succeed. It was what she lived for and why she'd become a Marine and a secret operative.

She adjusted her veil and then the traditional garments worn by Pakistani women. They were in Kabul, about to enter an event at a local meeting center and hotel. Their surveillance team was in position at the venue with eyes on four main members of a terrorist cell who surprisingly had ties to the United States. What they'd uncovered in the last twenty-four hours had Washington demanding proof and some exact locations of weapons of mass destruction and militant training facility locations. Sacha was going in to confirm, document, and basically identify other key players and locations while the team in the hotel and center kept watch on their suspects. She was going in with Charro, a very intense and valuable asset to their team. He knew where the office was they needed to infiltrate and where these microchips and thumb drives were.

The problem now was that Spence couldn't confirm the pickup spot for all of the team for one hour from now. She heard him yelling into the phone in the native language. Then he slammed it down as she prepared to leave. She looked at her watch. She was running out of time.

"I'm going. I'll wait for you guys where we planned."

"If something changes, and you're not there by eight, I'll get to Balochistan, and we'll meet up."

"Where?" She pushed the map to him. This hadn't been in the plans. What the heck? Before she could question it, he was pulling over the map. It was the wrong one. He was not good at this at all. She looked at the map and the location of the small town near the dessert and mountains. She pointed. "There. It's a small bus depot. Only gets a few busses in and out a day. Are you sure about this?"

He held her gaze. "Don't worry. Everything will end here in Kabul and we'll be on our way."

She nodded. "Good luck and see you in an hour." She headed out.

As she made her way along the streets, she kept her gaze down and wouldn't make eye contact with anyone. Five minutes later, she arrived at the building and entered the small gathering.

Her heart was racing, her palms sweaty, but her job was easy. She was a cover for Charro as he headed upstairs and did his thing.

As she came toward the meeting point, she waited and waited, but Charro never arrive. A quick glance at her watch and she knew the window of opportunity was closing. They needed those chips and thumb drives. She glanced around and inconspicuously climbed the stairs. She got to the office and pushed open the door. She was in a panic. Where had Charro said those thumb drives and chips were?

She glanced at the closed door and then headed to the desk. She looked though and then remembered something about a safe and a key in the top drawer of the desk.

She pulled it opened, got the key, and then looked around for the safe. Turning, pushing things aside, she saw the curtain and then a picture. It was crooked. Could it be?

Her hands were shaking as she lifted the picture and saw the safe behind it. She carefully placed the picture on the floor and then used the key to open the safe.

"Bingo," she whispered, seeing the thumb drives, the microchips, and an envelope with more stuff in it, plus gold. She closed up the safe, put the picture back on the wall, and was placing the key into the drawer when she heard something going on right outside of the door.

She stuffed the envelope into her shirt under the gown. She reached for her gun and got down low behind the desk. She was going to get caught. She was going to die here and so was the rest of the team if she didn't get these things out of here and to a safe location.

The door opened, and three men came barreling in, holding Charro. They started slugging him and yelling at him in their language. She heard what they were saying. That they knew about the others at the party, that they were dead, and he was next.

They said something about another agent and wanted to know where the thumb drives were. What other agent?

Charro was trying to resist them, and then she made her move.

"Let him go," she yelled at them.

The one guy turned to shoot, and instinctively, she shot him. The next guy went to shoot, and she shot him, and then Charro got the third guy around the neck from behind and snapped his neck. He fell to the ground.

"Did you get the stuff?"

"Yes."

"Let's get the fuck out of here. It's just us, Sacha. The others are dead."

"Are you sure?" she asked as he took the guns from the guys and handed her one of them.

"Yes. Someone gave up the operation and identified the others. We need to get the hell out of here."

As they headed down the hallway, men appeared and started shooting. She and Charro shot back, blasting their way through them and down the back stairs. They exited to the outside and heard the yelling, people pointing and giving up their location. They ran faster and then went into the darkness.

"What do we do? Head back to the meeting spot?"

"We check it out first. Don't show our faces. They could be watching. My cover's blown," he said to her when suddenly the street where they were lit up with gunshots as men came running out of the building.

She and Charro fired. They took out a few of them, and then Charro said to run. She did as he said, and they ran for blocks and then headed toward the crowds of people in the streets and the vendors selling items.

People screamed, trying to get out of the way of gunfire. She followed Charro and kept on him close. It was only them. They ran so fast and came around on the other side of the street vendors.

"We should backtrack and see if the others made it, just in case." He looked at his watch. "We have five minutes to get to the meeting spot for the pickup."

"Okay. Whatever you think."

He grabbed her shoulders and shook her. "We were set up. I didn't get halfway down the hallway before those guys came out and grabbed me."

"How do you think they found out?" she asked him.

He released her arms. "Come on," he said, and she followed. They stayed close to the walls and in the shadows. "It had to be someone on the inside."

They approached the end of the buildings where the street corner was. A block down the way was the bus terminal. It was crowded and hard to make out the individual people.

"I don't see anyone, do you?" he asked her.

She was looking all over and at all the faces. "It's too damn crowded."

He looked at her. "Put the veil up. Cover yourself good." He rechecked his weapon, put in a new clip, and she did the same with hers. She had one additional clip on her.

Charro stared down into her eyes. He cupped her cheek. "I should have spoken to you sooner about getting out of this shit."

She squinted at him, not understanding what he was saying but feeling that attraction she always had to Charro. They spoke often on the downtimes, about his friends, about how he wanted her to meet them. The things he said, and hinted about, were intriguing, but could she give up being a Marine, a special operations intelligence officer?

"When this is done, you and I are going to explore these feelings we've both been ignoring. Then I'm taking you to meet my family."

She was shocked at his words, at the sincerity in his voice and in his eyes, but just as quickly as he hit her with this revelation that she knew, when he said family, he meant his three best friends, he got back to business.

"Let's get a closer look."

Her heart was pounding, the adrenaline still pumping from the earlier shootout. If they got caught, if those soldiers found them, they would be killed. No question. She trusted Charro. She'd realized just how much at this moment when he expressed how deeply he cared and also planned on getting them to safety, together. She sucked up the fear, the gut instinct that warned her to not go into the crowd but head away from here. Far, far away from here. But they would never leave a man behind. They had to ensure that no one was left from the team and in need of help.

She hurried along with him, weapon in hand, covered by the garment she wore. They began to walk amongst the travelers.

She was hoping to catch a glimpse of Spence, Johnny, Carl, or even Cecile, anyone from the team of undercover operatives.

"Fuck. Run, Sacha. Run!" he yelled, drew his weapon, and fired.

She jerked at the sight as his head flew back and his body hit the ground. People screamed. She saw the bullet hole in his forehead. Her heart caught in her throat as she froze in place and stared down at him. This wasn't real. He wasn't dead. The yelling and commotion caused her to snap out of her shock as she looked and saw the men, three of them with guns. Then they looked at her, and the veil fell from her mouth, revealing her American identity and the makeshift disguise to be fake, and it was as though they weren't sure if she was with Charro or not. Then they spoke in their language. "You, right there. Don't move." She started to ease her way back. They yelled stop, and she turned and ran.

They were following her. Charro was dead, killed right next to her as they searched for their team. Everyone must be dead. She was totally freaking out, scared out of her mind, stuck in this godforsaken country with no other help or contacts. Bullets whizzed past her head as she ducked around the corner, pulled her weapon, turned, and shot. Once, twice. She took two down, and the third jumped for cover. She took off running, down the side streets, between the crowds of locals selling vegetables, handmade products, food, clothing. There were so many people and then sets of five-story buildings. She headed toward the back of the buildings where the high grasses were and lots of brush and places to hide.

She was shaking so hard as she turned and ducked down low behind some heavy brush. She could hear him. He was yelling into a radio, saying that she was in the brush somewhere and that he needed backup.

Charro was dead. Everyone is dead except for me. What the fuck went wrong?

She remembered Charro's words. "We were set up. Someone from the inside."

She thought of his admission, his idea of them exploring their feelings for one another and meeting his family. His family was a bunch of soldiers, too. She wanted to cry, to scream in anger at what had just happened. They'd killed Charro. A bullet to his head right next to her.

Sacha covered her mouth with her hand, and it was too late when she felt the presence and then the body slam against hers. She lost her breath, felt the heavy clothing, the weapons, and the belt of bullets along his jacket. It was the man who'd been chasing them. She forearmed him to the throat. He struck her back. She was screaming and yelling in anger, in desperation, and tried to maneuver her weapon into position to shoot him. He grabbed her clothing, ripped it, and struck her again and again. Her arm was stuck under the garment she wore as her disguise. She cursed the damn thing and then felt his hands rip open the robe, tearing it and freeing her arms. She gripped her weapon.

She head-butted him. His nose broke, and blood splattered. He yelled at her in his language, telling her she was a whore, a dead American whore, and that she would die just like the others, that Black Out could never be stopped.

"Fuck you." She shifted her knee up, sending him upward. She heard the yelling and him telling backup where they were. She didn't want to die. She wasn't going to die here. Images of her father and her brother popped into her head. She was a Marine, a fighter, well trained, and she would die for her country. Black Out would not win. She pulled the trigger of her gun, hitting him in the gut, sending him off of her as she rolled to the right. The others were on her, just feet away as she shifted up, shooting from a sitting position, using her stomach and leg muscles to remain upright as she picked them off one after the next. Six men and then she felt the hit to her side. She gasped as the seventh jumped toward her, firing his weapon, and she just kept shooting. It was like slow motion, watching him fly through the air, feeling the bullet to her side penetrate her skin, and then seeing his body jerk simultaneously as he fell right over her and she used her legs and arms to flip him.

She slammed backward, landed hard to the ground, felt the ache and the loss of breath, but her adrenaline was pumping, and she was determined to live. She scooted out from under him and looked around in the darkness, barely seeing the bodies. In the distance she heard more yelling, and she knew she wouldn't be able to hold them off. The sight of the blood on a face drew her closer. The disguise had been lifted from his face and revealed a white man. An American?

She pulled herself up, grabbed her side, took two other guns and ammo, and ran. She just kept running and running until she could no longer catch her breath and her legs gave up on her.

* * * *

"Franco, I understand that you're upset. We all are, but you can't just take off for Kabul and Pakistan looking aimlessly for your sister. It's been eight weeks since we were notified of her disappearance and possible death. Eight weeks," Maddox Landers said to Franco as Franco paced.

Franco exhaled as he stood there waiting to leave for his own special operations mission in Iraq. Maddox had been forthright in showing him all the files, the pictures they'd gotten from intelligence and droids showing how brutally Sacha's team had been murdered. Her body hadn't been found. No one had reported any sightings of an American woman on the run, or being found dead, or even attempting to get into an embassy. Could they be holding her prisoner? The thought angered him and put a fear in his gut like nothing else.

Maddox came around his desk. The man was older with gray hair and dark glasses, and he was a bit of a prick. He had a great reputation, and Franco had been pleased when Sacha wound up in a special unit under his command. He hadn't realized the intense and dangerous shit she had been doing, but that was Sacha. She lived on the edge, always had something to prove, and she was capable. He'd take her as a teammate and partner in any mission he went on, no matter how dangerous. Their father had taught them well. He'd drilled in survival techniques, self-defense, and psychological strength training so they would be more than prepared if ever held prisoner by the enemy.

While other girls were playing with dolls and thinking about first kisses and dates, she was kicking boys' asses in hand-to-hand combat, assembling and disassembling her weapon in record speed, and earning respect and commendations from all her commanding officers and her fellow Marines. She was an asset to the Corps and to the United States of America. But what the fuck was she doing in Kabul in the middle of all this danger and terrorist shit?

"It's frustrating, Maddox. From what you've been so kind to share with me, it seems like it was a set-up. Are you guys investigating any leads as to who snitched on them or screwed up the intel?"

Maddox exhaled and ran his hand along his jaw. "I'm going to be honest with you and give you it straight, but if you say a word, I'll deny ever even speaking to you, never mind showing you the pictures."

He nodded.

"From what's being gathered so far, it looks like Charro or Spencer set the team up."

He squinted at him. He knew who Charro was. In fact, he knew some men who were good friends with Charro and had even worked with him. The Vancouver men had gone on missions with Charro. There was no way Charro was involved.

"I doubt Charro had anything to do with it. He's good people, a true American soldier and patriot. There's no way."

"Well, our investigators are gathering evidence. So far they've come up with some possible incriminating evidence on both Charro and Spence."

"Like what?"

"Like I cannot get into it. I'm sorry, Franco."

Franco exhaled. "I understand. Please keep me informed of any news or changes. I want to be kept abreast of the investigation so that justice can be served."

"I understand. Your sister was a major asset to the team." He reached out to shake his hand. Franco shook it, holding it and holding Maddox's gaze.

"My sister isn't dead. I just know she isn't."

Maddox gave him a somber expression and didn't argue or reply. Franco headed out of the office feeling angry, useless, and ready to blow his stack. He made his way out of the federal building and headed toward the parking garage. He was set to leave tonight. He needed to stop by his father's place and let him know what was going on now and who they were looking at.

* * * *

"Charro is a good soldier. There is no way he set the team up, and definitely not Sacha."

"Dad, I don't know what to believe. This not knowing is fucking killing me, and I need to leave for Iraq."

"And you will leave because you have a job to do. Maddox knows to contact me with any updates?"

Franco nodded.

"Good, so tell me what he gave you. What do they think went down and happened to the team?" Devan asked his son.

As he listened and heard about the multiple bodies and how the team had been tortured or killed execution style, he realized that it did seem as though the team had been set up. That someone who knew very intricate details of the mission had compromised it.

"It sounds like a set-up. There's no way it was Charro. What do we know about this Spence guy?"

"I couldn't find out much without raising red flags. I could already get into some serious trouble with what I snooped around looking for. That's how I got Maddox to give up more about the investigation."

"The waiting and not knowing if she is dead or alive is killing me, too. I'd hate to think that she is dead, but knowing where she was, and how impossible it would be to get across Pakistan and to India or a safer location for help, with no assistance or backup, leaves me to believe she's dead."

Devan felt sick to his stomach. She was his baby girl, his everything, and despite him teaching her to be self-sufficient and her being well trained in every aspect of being a soldier, an undercover operative, he wasn't prepared for these feelings of being useless and having to live without ever seeing her again. She was the last reminder of Ava, his wife who'd died in a car accident when Sacha was four. He didn't know anything about raising a girl, a child, but he'd done his best. She was eager to please, a smart, fast learner, and a sponge for military things, both history and being a soldier. He'd been her role model, and she'd instinctively idolized him and wanted to be just like him and, of course, like her big brother, Franco. They did everything together, and she never backed down. If she failed at something, she kept trying and trying until she got it right. She was a fighter.

The sound of Franco's phone ringing brought Devan's mind back to the present.

"Hello?" he answered.

His son covered his one ear, squinted, and raised his voice into the mouth of the phone.

"Long distance from who?" His son's eyes widened as he stared at Devan. "Sacha?"

Chapter 1

Sacha lay in a shitty bed in the middle of a shithole in New Delhi, India. She felt like hell. She was thin, battered still, but at least the bullet that had hit her side had gone right through the skin and not needed anything more than some stitches. She had waited until she was able to get into India and one of the clean clinics in town. She didn't even know what day it was until she finally got through the clinic, cleaned up a little, and into a spare room some locals rented out to her. Thank God she wore that military watch and the stupid gold ankle bracelet under her garments. She'd sold them all for cash, along with one of the guns and bullets she had, too. They were U.S. issued and worth a lot of money on the streets in Balochistan before she headed into Pakistan and then caught a ride into New Delhi. She didn't trust anyone and traveled on foot or stole vehicles when she could. She was surprised at her capabilities, but fear was a powerful motivator indeed.

She wouldn't head to the U.S. embassy because she didn't trust anyone. Someone had set them up and could be watching, just waiting to pick her off, especially since she was the sole survivor from the mission and she had the copies of the thumb drives and microchips. She'd watched Charro die right next to her, and she could have been killed, too.

She was pissed. She had so much time to think things through and realized that, perhaps, the snitch wasn't someone who was on the mission but someone who knew they were there in Kabul and ready to get evidence on Black Out and their terrorist operations. Could that small cell not be as small as the government thought? Why would someone in the U.S. not want to destroy such an organization? Her mind went over everything, and she figured it was better to be safe than sorry and not trust anyone. But she needed out of the Middle East. She needed to be on U.S. soil. Besides, she had the microchips, the thumb drives, and the other shit in this envelope that was encoded, whatever it was.

When she racked her brain trying to figure out whom to trust and who she didn't want to place in any danger, she came up short. The only people she trusted at the moment were her brother and father. Her dad was retired and older. He didn't need this kind of aggravation. Her brother, Franco, was still active duty, but she didn't want him involved. He could lose his position in the military or get killed trying to help her. But she really didn't have much of a choice. She was running out of money and had only about a week's worth of dough left. She needed out of here, and the only one who could help her was her brother. He could get fake passports, money, and get her a ride home.

She had made the call over a week ago and made him promise to not come here himself, especially because he had his own mission to go on. She didn't want any red flags raised or for anyone in the government to know she was back. Now all she could do was wait to see whom he sent to get her then pray that they made it out of here alive and that she had enough physical strength to get through the trek and finally make it home. Whoever was coming, she prayed they got here soon. She was tired of feeling scared.

* * * *

Damien placed the phone on speaker. His brothers, Elwood and Toro, gathered around him in their home office in Wellington. They were getting ready to head out to Crossroads for a few drinks with their friends.

"Holy shit, Franco. She's the only one alive?" he asked as Franco explained about the call from his sister, Sacha. A month ago they had found out that Charro, a very good friend of theirs, had been killed while on a mission. They had spoken to him only days earlier about him coming back home.

"Yes. The others are dead. Sacha is the only one who survived somehow. I couldn't get the details because time is limited and I'm shipping off to Iraq in about two hours. I need your help. No one can know where you're going or that you have Sacha."

Damien and his brothers listened as Franco explained about a snitch on the inside and setting them up. "Sacha explained briefly about not trusting anyone, not even her commanders. She also said going home, heading toward our father's, could be dangerous."

Damien knew she would need help getting into the States and would need fake I.D. and a passport.

"She should stay here with us, in Wellington. We have the cabin in the woods, which is secure, and have a high-tech security system in place. We can provide her with whatever she needs here." Elwood said, adding to the conversation.

"I was hoping that you would offer. I won't be back for four weeks, and my dad has respected Sacha's wishes for him to stay put and not show a change in his routine, just in case someone is watching."

"Jesus, your old man must be pissed," Toro said.

"He's relieved that she's alive. That's what we're focused on. You should know that she's injured. She didn't say how badly, but I heard the strain in her voice. She's been on the run, hiding, surviving for over a month's time. I know you guys, just like I do, have experience with coping after such an ordeal. She's stubborn."

"Like another Marine we know," Damien said, glancing at Toro.

"Yeah, well, she's extra stubborn and always having something to prove. She won't trust you. She may even think of leaving there because she wouldn't want to place you guys in danger, and I didn't exactly tell her that you guys were coming for her. The conversation was quick. God knows, when Sacha gets something in her head, there's no changing her mind about it. So this is what I think will work, if you can be prepared to head out ASAP."

Two hours later, Damien and his men were on route across the country, heading to the Middle East. He hoped they all got out of there alive.

* * * *

"They are no longer a problem, Mahem. I've told you to move on and finish the plan for the attack," he said to Mahem as he looked around at the buildings, being sure to use the untraceable burner phone.

"I put you in charge of this, and you weren't fully prepared to kill all of them."

"I didn't think they would get so close."

"Well, they did, and somehow that woman got her hands on things she should not have. I want you to find her. If she is alive, if she got out, then she has those documents and my entire operation, and your involvement, as well as the others', will be compromised. They'll be no covering this up."

He ran his fingers through his hair. He'd fucked up. Who would have thought that Charro and the team would have been so capable? Never mind that woman. He knew of the family. They were full-blooded Marine Corps, gung ho all the way.

"I have my eyes on the family of the soldier who is missing. If they make contact with her, and the brother and father make a move, I'll know it."

"You'd better. We need those thumb drives and microchips."

"So you're saying that my name, my involvement, is indicated on those? That everything I've helped you with thus far is all documented on there? How fucking stupid to put all of that on record."

"Not stupid, securing your part. That you would pull through on what you said you were capable of. I warn you now, screw this up and it won't matter what's on those thumb drives. You'll be dead," Mahem told him, and then the phone disconnected.

"Fuck. What the hell, Sacha? Where the fuck are you, and how in God's name did you survive?" He took the phone and placed it into his pocket. He'd destroy it soon enough. What he needed to do now was make a connection with his contacts. Something had to give. But how the hell could he try to locate her in the Middle East without raising any red flags as to why he was searching?

He thought about her brother. Word was he'd been asking and pushing for answers, for some indication as to what had gone down six weeks ago and why they didn't know who was responsible. The best thing that could happen would be for her to die. Then the heat would be off all of them. He wouldn't have to be worried about going to jail for the rest of his life for treason and for helping a terrorist cell pull off one major attack on U.S. soil. An attack that would take out multiple key senators and some highly powerful businessmen and women. It was a strategic opportunity for all involved, and because he would be so close when it happened, he would have the perfect excuse to head into early retirement, and with a nice, comfy security blanket of four million dollars.

He smiled as he headed back across the gardens and to the office building. *One female Marine is not going to ruin everything I've worked for. She is as good as dead, and anyone who helps her will die, too.*

* * * *

Sacha was in pain. From what she gathered from the village doctor, she had broken ribs, one of them cracked because of the bullet that had gone clean through it. She worried about infection, but that damn watch and one gun had gotten her a lot of money to work with, to get the best treatment she could in this little fucking village. Now that she was in New Delhi, the conditions were better, but she didn't take a chance at staying in some nicer hotel. She, instead, rented a bedroom from a landlord with multiple rooms in one dwelling. She got antibiotic cream to ensure keeping infection away. She took the room in the back, the one she could escape from in an emergency, or in case someone figured out where she was. She didn't even know what day it was. She didn't care because it would only anger her more that she'd been stuck here so long. Even though it beat the other alternative. Death.

She couldn't sleep, just little cat naps as exhaustion won out and then pain awoke her, as did the fear of being caught. They had to be looking for her. She'd killed all those men. She'd screwed up their plans, and she had the thumb drives. She wondered what was on them. What had been so important that a whole team of operatives, agents, and other men had to be killed to get these damn things? She shivered just thinking about what her future held. Was it even worth it to head to the States? Should she keep traveling and get lost somewhere? She went over all the alternatives, but truth was she would never feel safe. She would always have that uneasy feeling in her gut as if someone was watching her or on her trail.

At least on U.S. soil, she could regroup, build her strength, figure out whom to trust, and get mentally and physically ready for what may come. It was better than sitting here rotting, running out of money and a source to pay for food and care. She had no choice. She needed her brother's help, and it was a done deal. He was sending help.

She wondered when the team would arrive and whom exactly Franco would trust so much to send for her. As she lay on the bed, drifting off to sleep, her gun in hand, she heard something. It was dark outside. She didn't dare move a muscle as she remained with gun in hand. When the door creaked open, she aimed, ready to shoot and kill, and use her last few bullets if necessary.

"Sacha?"

She heard her name.

"Identify yourself or I put a bullet in your fucking head."

"We're friendlies, Marines sent by Franco as planned." He came into view from behind the door. Extralarge, dressed in black. He approached slowly. He looked at her, and she wished she were in better physical condition, stronger, cleaner, but she wasn't. She was a mess.

"It's going to be okay. Put down the gun so my team can come in here and assess your injuries before we get the fuck out of here."

She had to admit that hearing the thick Bronx accent made her think America, New York, safety, and courage. She lowered the gun.

He made a sound, and another huge guy came in, and then a third was by the door.

"Let's move. I don't like this spot. We're wide open," the guy at the door said.

"How bad are your injuries?" one asked as he squatted down by the bed and reached out to push up her top. She grabbed his hand, as his fingers grazed over the envelope, the only bit of evidence and clues she had as to who had killed Charro and the rest of the team, what she'd risked her life for and killed to keep in her possession.

"I'm fine. I can make it. What's the plan?" She lifted up, losing her breath a little because her ribs were so badly bruised still and healing. He helped her.

"We have to walk on foot a few blocks, and then we have a vehicle that we'll drive to a place to get you cleaned up and looking like a tourist." She locked onto his dark-blue eyes, and she realized who he was. Charro had begun to share some info about them. He showed her a picture of them, and she remembered the man with the dark blue eyes. He told her about the team he had been part of for years until he was asked to be part of this mission over a year ago. He had described them. Why would Franco send them?

"Vancouver?" she asked in a whisper.

"Yes. Now let's move. The faster we get you out of here and cleaned up, the faster we can get you to the States."

* * * *

Elwood held his gun and watched Damien talking to Sacha and helping her to get up off the bed. She looked weak and exhausted, and he knew she had been through hell just by the sight of her, never mind by the info they had thus far. As she started to take some steps, she faltered.

"Let me carry you," Damien said.

"No way," she snapped, determined to not lean on him or be carried.

She was stubborn, and as they got out of the building and started walking along the pathway, they spotted some older man, and he looked concerned. When Damien went to point his gun, Sacha stopped him and then spoke to the man in his language. The man looked at the four of them and then nodded, placed his hands together, and bowed at her, wishing them luck.

"He was a help to me."

By the time they got her to the small hotel and were able to get her upstairs, she was spent. Damien laid her down on the bed.

"Rest."

"What is the plan?" she asked as Elwood and Toro stood by, holding their guns, remaining on guard. She looked from one of them to the next.

"Our flight out of here is early morning. It will take us about an hour drive to get there."

"We'll cut it too close if I rest now. We'll all feel a lot safer if we're closer to the airport and ready to leave."

"You can hardly stand, Sacha. A thirty-minute rest will be a good thing," Damien said to her.

"No, we're in a hotel room. There's no way to escape easily, and I won't put you in that kind of danger. We need to keep moving and get the hell out of here." She went to stand and teetered on her feet. Damien grabbed her.

"We're staying here and getting you cleaned up. You'll need to get through security at the airport without showing any signs of injury and fatigue. You need to do this our way," he said firmly.

She looked at him and exhaled. "Fine. But I'll just get showered and cleaned up. We can wait closer to the airport. It will be safer."

"You won't be able to stand up to shower and clean yourself. We wait," Damien told her firmly.

"No. Just help me get showered and presentable."

Toro swallowed hard.

Damien looked to them then back at her.

"You want me to help you shower?" he asked, sounding shocked from Toro's perspective. Toro was shocked, too. She really wanted out of here. She was so scared.

"Get everything set up in the bathroom. Then, Elwood, you go down and get some food while Toro stands guard and keeps watch. I'll help Sacha so we can leave sooner."

Elwood nodded, and he could tell that Damien wasn't too happy about having to do this, but it would be better for them to get closer to the airport, wait there, and make sure the I.D. worked properly, and then they could all head back to the U.S. By the time they landed in New Jersey, they would have explained to her, on the five-hour road trip up north, where her new residence would be for quite some time.

* * * *

Damien helped her get into the bathroom. The shower was running, thanks to Toro, who'd returned to the bedroom. Damien had rolled up his sleeves and tested the water. Sacha stood in front of him. Her eyes were glazed over with exhaustion, and dark circles surrounded the bold sage-green color of her eyes. She wasn't the same woman he'd seen in the pictures Charro had sent them. In those pictures, she was stunning, well endowed, and her eyes made her look capable of anything. She was a fighter and that was obvious by her standing here, surviving the ordeal. They would get the full story as soon as they were safe. He couldn't help but to wonder if Charro had been sleeping with her. Recently, he'd mentioned getting out and bringing Sacha along with him to visit Wellington. He'd hinted at things.

She unbuttoned the top, and he saw the small yellow envelope, dirty, crinkled. He reached for it.

"What's this?" he asked, and she squeezed her hand over his. She held his gaze.

"This stays on me at all times. This is going to help me find who killed Charro and the rest of my team. I won't give this up to anyone. Friend of Charro, Franco, or not. Got it?" she said fiercely.

He squinted at her. No one spoke to him like that, but he understood she was fearful, desperate to feel safe. Her brother was right. She wouldn't trust them fully, not for quite some time or until they'd proved themselves trustworthy.

"Well, you can't shower with it. Let me put it right here. It's close by, and no one will touch it."

She stared at him, looking up into his eyes. She had to be about five feet seven. He still towered over her at six foot three. Her long brown blonde hair was a mess of strands and knots.

She nodded and let her fingers fall from the envelope, and he placed it down onto the toilet cover, where she could see it clearly.

She closed her eyes and teetered a moment. He grabbed her hips and felt her hipbones, and she popped her eyes open.

"Let's get you cleaned up, get some food in you, and head home, Sacha. I promise my team and I can get you to safety. Trust me."

"It's not about trust. Prove yourself and get me out of here," she said, so stone faced and serious that he knew she was going to need some serious counseling or, at least, a minimum amount of time to process what she'd gone through and how she'd survived while everyone else died.

He slowly moved his hands toward the buttons on the blouse. He undid them and pulled it off of her gently. She was cut up, defined with muscles, and despite being so thin, her breasts were full and filled the tank top she had on underneath. He reached for the hem and looked into her eyes. She was in a zone. He knew that look. She was focused, thinking about something else and trying to cope with having to have him, a strange man, a fellow Marine, wash her, see her naked, and give him that trust she was fighting with every last ounce of energy she probably had right now.

"Let's make this quick and painless." He lifted her tank top up and over her head. Her breasts bounced. Her injuries came into view, and he clenched his teeth.

"Jesus, what the fuck?" he asked as he looked closer at her wound. It was a decent stitch job of stitches but there was also massive discoloration along all her ribs and side up to her breast.

"Took a bullet to the side. Went straight through the rib, or in between, I don't know. It was hard to understand what the doctor was explaining. All my ribs were bruised or broken. Probably from the ground fight." She closed her eyes and teetered again.

Ground fight? Jesus, what the fuck did she go through?

"Let's get this skirt off and get you in the shower. You'll feel better with new clothes."

She nodded, and he pushed down her skirt and panties.

He helped her into the shower, trying his hardest not to look at her curves, at the way her belly sank in and her ribs stuck out, or the way her ass, muscular and small, tilted outward.

He began to lather up the soap as she stood under the spray of hot water. She had her head down, and he reached for the shampoo and then began to wash her hair, massaging her scalp. She moaned and gasped a little, indicating there were other injuries, but she was trying not to show pain. He washed her up using the washcloth and the soap to clean her. She reached for the cloth and helped best as she could. When he was done, he helped squeeze her long brownish-blonde hair out and then reached for the towel. When she turned to look at him, face cleaner, hair washed and wet, her light sage green eyes held his as he wrapped her into the towel and lifted her up to place her feet onto the small towel on the bathroom floor so he could dry her.

"I owe you one, Vancouver."

He swallowed hard as he began to dry her body as she finger combed her hair.

"We grabbed what we could and what we thought would look best as a tourist traveling here. You're a lot thinner than we expected."

"Whatever it is, it will be fine because it's clean and it isn't local attire," she said.

"I didn't know the size for undergarments."

"I don't even care," she whispered, and he reached for a sports bra and helped her get it on. She adjusted her breasts in it, and it was way too small, but she made do considering her ribs ached as she squeezed into it.

He helped her with the panties. Then he placed the long-sleeve dress over her head and helped her get it into place. "We got a sweater, too, and a backpack with some other clothes so it doesn't look suspicious."

She nodded.

He was compelled to help her feel safe, to get her through this. He felt different, protective beyond this being a job, a mission for Charro and for Franco. Maybe because he'd seen her naked, at her most vulnerable, he took it seriously and as a sign of trust, whether Sacha thought of it like that or not.

"We'll get you to safety. We have your six, Marine."

Her eyes filled up with emotion, and she swallowed, and that indication of vulnerability disappeared. All she did was nod, and then he helped her walk out of the bathroom to sit on the bed. Toro handed her some food.

He would get her to the States and keep her safe in Wellington, and then he would find out exactly what she'd gone through, how Charro had died, and what was in the envelope that could answer all their questions and bring justice to all of those who were killed.

Chapter 2

Sacha spent the first week sleeping and trying to regain her strength. She forced herself to do sit-ups and push-ups every morning and every night. She hadn't been happy about this plan that her brother and the Vancouver men had come up with, but it made sense. No one knew them. No one knew of this cabin in the woods, and the men ensured her that they had no visitors.

She tried making a plan in her head, now that she was feeling stronger, and eating three meals a day. She had yet to speak to her father, and the men informed her that her brother was in Iraq on a mission for a month. Even when he returned to the States, she wouldn't let him come here. Whoever set up her and the team would know all about them and their families. The last thing she needed was for her brother or father to get caught in the middle of this and get killed.

She thought about Damien, Elwood, and Toro. The more alert she became as time passed, the more she saw in them. Now that she had strength and could take care of herself, she felt embarrassed about having had Damien bathe her multiple times. He was a large man with a fierce, unapproachable expression on his face. It had been on the third day she was here that, while he was helping her, she'd seen a change in that expression, and in the way he stroked his fingers below her rib as he checked her injuries. The way he eased her gently into the bathtub, taking his time to release her as he set her down. He insisted upon washing her hair, caressing her skin with the soapy washcloth, and she felt something was happening between them and fast. She sensed this connection, something she was refusing to acknowledge for so many reasons. For such a muscular, tough soldier of a man, he had been gentle, patient, and even seemed disappointed when she told him she was stronger and could handle showering by herself. That care, that connection, made him stand guard outside her door and wait to ensure she didn't need help.

She avoided him now, like she avoided Elwood and Toro for similar reasons. In her mind, in times like now, when she was bored and refused to go downstairs to be near them because that would mean talking to them and showing emotion, she would think about Charro. His words, his expression, the feel of his hand against her cheek as he explained his hope for them when they finished the mission. She swallowed hard.

He'd wanted to explore their feelings. He'd wanted to bring her here to meet these men, his family, as he thought of them, and she couldn't help but to wonder why. Then she started to wonder if Charro had told Damien, Elwood, and Toro his intentions and wondered what they thought about it.

She thought about Elwood. Only about an inch shorter than Damien, Elwood was filled with energy. He couldn't seem to stand still long, and she noticed, throughout their journey from New Delhi, that it was Elwood who ran the errands, was two steps ahead of the next thing, and always eager to move on to the next thing. It wasn't until he was on the plane and sitting beside her that he finally slowed down and sat watch. She didn't think he slept, but she wouldn't know. She'd conked out and awoken on Damien's shoulder a few times and then Elwood's shoulder, too.

A glance at Toro, and the serious, firm expression as he watched her, told her he was in tune to the vibes surrounding them, and it was as if he had something to say but held back. It was just another reason to stay upstairs.

She walked over to the window and looked between the small gap in the curtain and into the woods. She wouldn't open it, wider despite the gorgeous view and privacy of the forest. She was too scared and thought that someone could be watching her from a distance, waiting to strike. It kept her on edge.

She gasped when she heard the knock and kicked herself for not even hearing the footsteps coming down the hallway.

She stood still, ran her palms down the tight jeans, and adjusted the long-sleeve cotton shirt in burgundy.

"Come in," she whispered.

She was a bit surprised to see Toro there. She'd expected Damien. He seemed to be the one who took charge of checking in on her.

"What's going on?" he asked.

She stared up at him. He was the tallest of the three men. He must be at least six foot four. He glanced at her and then the window then back at her.

"It's nice out. You should open the curtains and let the light in."

"No thank you."

"Is there a problem?" he asked in an abrupt tone as if he were annoyed with her.

She'd realized pretty quickly that Toro had a chip on his shoulder and might be the kind of Marine, and man, who didn't think fondly of women in the Corps. She didn't know why she felt that way, but maybe it had something to do with the way he looked at her when Damien needed to help her shower or perhaps how he watched her avoid the game room where there were pictures of their friends, including Charro, and she just couldn't look at them yet. She wasn't sure, but the man put her on edge and made her worry.

"It's safe here, Sacha, to have the blinds open. There isn't anyone out there watching you. We have extra surveillance video and motion sensors hooked up to a high-tech system around the perimeter and throughout the house. If there's a fucking chipmunk climbing along the tree, we fucking know about it." He walked over, opened the curtains and raised the blinds higher.

She fought the urge to hide. Instead, she walked closer to the bedroom door. When he left, she would close it.

He looked at her and let his eyes roam over her from head to toe. The clothes they'd gotten her were tight. They knew nothing about shopping for a woman. But it could be worse, and she could be swimming in the clothes. At least them being tight made her watch her calorie intake, considering her exercise regimen was slimmed down some.

He glanced at the window and then back at her.

"It's normal to feel paranoid and on edge after escaping being killed. You went through a lot. Although you have yet to share the details with us, it seems that way. It will pass, and when you're ready to talk, we will listen." He sounded so robotic and rehearsed.

"Having a gun would be nice."

"Not happening. You need to recover. We need to arrange for some sort of counseling to help you get through the ordeal."

"I don't need counseling. I need to get organized and regroup. I need to have a look into the thumb drives and files on a secure, untraceable system, and alone. Then I need to figure out who these assholes are and take them down."

"Well, that's not happening for quite some time."

"It will happen when I say it happens," she snapped at him.

He looked at her with an expression that totally said she'd gone over the line, and she lowered her eyes automatically. Toro was that damn intimidating and confident. Plus, him and the others outranked her. She automatically realized that, even though they weren't technically in charge of her and that she wasn't on a government mission with them, there was still that respect for authority and higher power. All three men were more capable than her. She knew it. But the need to remain independent as much as possible and strong was overwhelming. Toro had the instant ability to get under her skin.

"Every day you'll get stronger. You'll see," he said to her and then walked closer.

She stared at him, and he just looked down at her with those dark-blue eyes and an all-knowing expression. It was as though he understood what she was feeling and going through. He'd seen combat. He'd looked death in the eyes and escaped it. More than once. She knew it instantly.

"Ready for lunch?"

"I guess so," she said, not wanting to stand here alone with him. He weakened her resolve to be strong and alone. He challenged her with very little words. It was intimidating, and she didn't care for it one bit. She got back her attitude. They walked out of the bedroom, and he followed her down the stairs.

As they walked, she glanced back at him.

"So basically what you're telling me is that you think I'll emotionally lose my mind, like some post-traumatic stress situation, and I'll try to sneak into your bedrooms at night and kill you and your team if I have access to a gun?" she asked, hearing the sarcasm in her own voice as she stopped at the bottom of the stairs.

He stopped right behind her. She could feel his large presence and the warmth of his body, too. She looked over her shoulder at him.

"You could never sneak up on me or the team. Our worry is for you and doing something stupid."

He slid past her as she took the last step and then glanced toward the kitchen.

"I may be a little off my game as I recover, but I'm certain it won't be long before I'm a hundred percent," she said to him as they entered the kitchen.

"You check her wound?" Damien asked as he set the cold cuts and bread down on the table for them to make sandwiches.

"Didn't get a chance, not enough light in the dungeon."

She shot Toro a dirty look, and Damien caught it. Elwood just stared at her as he stopped making a sandwich.

"Staying in the dark all day and night is not a good thing," Damien said to her.

"I'm catching up on my sleep." She held on to the top of the chair as she looked up at them watching her.

"You don't need to be afraid here. We've got your back. It's safe."

"I need to do this my way. Why don't you back off?"

She pulled out the chair and placed a knee on the seat as she reached for a roll but paused when she took the knife to cut it open. She glanced up at Toro. "Am I allowed to use the knife, or do you think I'll try slitting one of your throats or maybe my wrists with it?" she snapped at him but didn't wait for an answer as she lifted the knife and cut into the bread.

"What the hell is that supposed to mean?" Damien asked.

"Nothing," Toro snapped back and went about making his sandwich.

"Doesn't sound like nothing to me," Damien replied.

"She's just being emotional. Forget it and let her be," Toro said.

"Emotional? What the hell is that supposed to mean?" she snapped at him, dropping the knife onto the table and staring up at him across the table. Toro locked gazes with her, his expression intense and angry.

"You can't handle any bit of being taken care of and assisted in your recovery. You're on edge because you know you're not at the top of your game physically or mentally. We're trying to help you, but you're being a bi—"

"Enough," Damien said.

"No, not enough. I 'm trying to get my mind straight. I'm trying to regain strength."

"Then look at the damn pictures and mourn his loss," Toro yelled at her.

She looked at Elwood and Damien, who just stared at her. She knew Elwood and Toro were pissed because she couldn't, wouldn't, walk into the game room and look at the framed pictures of them and Charro together, of good times, of special moments in the military, but she couldn't do it.

"You're not in charge of me. You're not my commander," she said to Toro.

"No, he isn't, but I am, for the time being and under this controlled situation. Someone must maintain order and respect around here. I'm it. Let's settle down, eat some lunch, and then talk about this," Damien said.

"No." She turned around and headed out of the room and up the stairs.

She didn't know how this whole thing had gone so wrong, just like she didn't know how or why this conversation with Toro had turned into a pissing contest. Before she made it to her bedroom and could close the door, Damien was there. He shocked her, approaching from behind and standing there in the doorway.

She walked over to the curtains and shoved them closed. She turned around.

"Sacha?" He said her name and walked farther into the room.

"I don't know what his problem is. He started with me, and over the damn pictures, and saying I couldn't have a gun or I might hurt myself or try to hurt you guys because of post-traumatic stress. Do I fucking look like I'm suffering from PTSD?" She raised her voice, and he raised one of his eyebrows up at her. She went to say something as her mind processed her behavior and her outburst. She plopped down on the edge of the bed and growled as she ran her fingers through her hair.

"It's normal to feel this way. Maybe if you talked a little bit about what happened, it could make you feel better?"

She shook her head.

She didn't want to relive it. She had flashbacks at night when she slept and even during the day when she napped. She wasn't going to sit here and tell him about the mission going wrong and about watching a bullet hit Charro in the head.

"No," she whispered.

He walked closer. "You're being stubborn. We're not the bad guys."

She looked at him. Her chest tightened. She didn't trust anything or anyone, but she was feeling as if she could trust them, but then she thought about the mission. It was supposed to be pretty damn safe, aside from getting her hands on the thumb drives and microchips. She still hadn't looked at them yet.

"I know you're scared. You don't know who to trust or what do with the evidence, if it even is evidence as to who killed Charro and the team. But you need to know that we're not the enemy. We're here to help you. Your brother put your life in our hands, and we will protect you. If it makes you feel any better, Charro told us about you, a year ago."

She clasped her hands on her lap and looked up at him. She fought to remember Charro's words and what he'd told her. She didn't need to feel weak or be emotional like Toro accused her of being because she was a female.

"He never said a word about any of you," she said and looked away from him. Even after she said the words, it hurt and didn't feel right to lie to him. But she was confused. She was feeling things she wasn't used to and didn't want to face. She was attracted to Damian, to Toro, and Elwood. Charro wanted her to meet them. Charro wanted to explore his feelings for her and never had the chance. Now she was here, putting his family—his best friends—in danger and could get them killed, too. She felt guilty and conflicting about telling him she lied, and that Charro had told her about them. But when she sort of had the nerve to look back at him, she caught sight of his back as he left the room, closing the door behind him.

* * * *

"Should we go wake her or see if she wants to eat?" Elwood said as they sat at the kitchen table eating dinner.

"No. Let her be. She needs to work this through and to learn to trust us."

"I don't think that's going to happen, Damien," Toro said to him.

"You remember what Charro said to us over a year ago? How he talked about this woman, a fellow Marine that he was impressed with?" Damien asked.

"There's no need to even talk about it. It was farfetched, even with Charro," Toro snapped at him, then put another bite of food into his mouth and finished up his dinner. He pushed the plate forward. He glanced up toward the staircase. Still no sign of Sacha.

"It wasn't so farfetched when we sat here drinking beers and talking about retiring from all the dangerous bullshit," Damien added.

"Yeah, like that would happen. Even living out here we've had to assist with a few situations that required our expertise," Toro said.

"But it was for friends and this community. Any of us are always willing to help a woman in danger and her men," Elwood said to them.

"Franco chose us to go get her and bring her back safely. He trusts us with protecting her and helping her get through this and live. The fact that Charro told us his plan of bringing Sacha back here to the States and introducing us to her had meaning, too."

"Yeah, he bought into the idea of wanting to be normal. This whole concept of sharing a woman as a team because individually he wouldn't feel like he could succeed in being everything a woman needed," Toro said.

"It was more than that. We've seen it firsthand with our friends. With our friends, Riley, Chancellor, Tiegen, Mitch, and a bunch of other men who share one woman, protect her, and provide for her," Damien said to Toro.

"But this woman is Sacha. She's a Marine, a trained killer, and resourceful soldier. What the fuck does she need us for? Sex?" Toro asked.

"Damn, Toro, is your heart made of stone? How about to just understand and empathize with by what we experience in our professions? To get it and to know what it feels like to lose a fellow soldier, a best friend, and to see bad people do bad shit?" Elwood asked and then stood up and walked his plate to the sink.

"I don't know why we're talking about this now. It didn't work out. Charro didn't make it, and Sacha is afraid and unwilling to trust us even enough to talk about the evidence and tell us how her team died, how Charro died. I don't trust it," Toro said, rising from his seat. They didn't say another word about it. Everyone was in a state as they cleaned up then called it a night.

* * * *

They got her so angry. The three of them and their damn confidence and ability to be so strong. Was it just because she was a woman that she was feeling so emotional, angry, and wanting to scream? She didn't know, but as she tried to stay away from them and tried not to think about Kabul and about Charro, she just couldn't fight it any longer.

She needed to face the fear, the anger, and sadness at losing him the way she had. At never knowing if anything could have come of them exploring their attraction and him bringing her here to meet Toro, Damien, and Elwood under different terms. What did it mean? She heard that a lot of people, troops, shared their women. A team to one woman to cope with all they did and do as soldiers. She got it, understood it, but her mindset was different. Her father and the Corps had drilled into her head the need to survive solo when all else failed. Well, all else had failed. She was alone. She couldn't trust anyone and couldn't even follow her gut. That was another thing. She thought about that gut instinct now as she tiptoed down the stairs and toward the game room.

A whole other week had passed with her avoiding them as best she could, especially avoiding Toro.

When she and Charro had been in the city and moving toward the bus station to see if they could identify the others, she had the feeling that they shouldn't, but she'd put her trust in Charro as military leader. He had just confessed his desire to explore their attraction, her mind whirling with the what-ifs. *What if I said no? What if I begged him to just leave and get the hell out of Kabul together?*

She held on to the doorframe, trying to see in the darkness yet not quite ready to. She walked into the dark room and could see slightly with the light of the moon coming in. On the one wall were pictures of different events and activities in the military and civilian settings with Toro, Damien, Elwood, Charro, and even other troops and local friends.

It would be a glimpse into his life and perhaps some times they could have shared together would have been added to this wall.

She walked toward the small table and turned on the light. She didn't look up, couldn't look up, yet. She needed to get herself ready to see Charro's face, his smile, him in good spirits and not with a bullet to his forehead and his dark green eyes wide open in shock. She felt her eyes well up with tears. She gripped one arm of the single seater chair and opened her eyes. Charro, in uniform with his buddies. Charro smiling wide as he posed in front of a tank. Charro drinking beers and watching what looked like football at some tailgate party with a bunch of buddies. Charro, staring right at her, smiling, in uniform and happy like she wanted to remember him but couldn't. The tears spilled from her eyes, no matter how hard she fought to keep them back. She thought again about what he'd said to her and about what the future might have held. She thought of his inference to his friends, the three men who'd come to rescue her and sneak her out of the Middle East. Three military men, best friends of Charro. Men he wanted her to meet with him. Did he imagine the five of them together, being lovers, partners for however long a relationship like that could last? She didn't know and couldn't tell if she wanted that only because he was gone now and it was what he wanted, or was it because somehow he'd known that she would be attracted to Elwood, Damien, and Toro, just like she was attracted to Charro but denied it, focusing on her job and being a Marine first? Look what being a Marine first had gotten her.

On the run from terrorists, so much anger in her heart, in her soul. All she kept thinking about since she'd gotten here was seeking revenge and, ultimately, having to go back to the Middle East. She knew once she looked at those thumb drives and microchips that she was going to set her eyes on the goal, the kill. Tears filled her eyes once again as they locked onto more images, great, happy pictures of Charro. She closed her eyes, imagining his cologne, his masculinity, and the way he spoke with her in his last moments. His focus had been on getting them to safety and working together so he could take her here to Wellington. She knew that now, but then, in that moment, she refused to think about pleasantries and fantasies or any human connection and bond. Instead, she'd focused on staying alive. She thought about what it might be like to be Charro's lover, to give of her body to him and know it would be more. It would be her soul, and she would never turn back. But that chance was gone now. All she had left of him were these pictures, these three men, and that memory of what he'd said to her, as well as the images of his death.

She closed her eyes and saw his head go back then his body hit the ground. Right before the bullet hit him, he'd looked at her, knowing his fate. Fear, like she had never seen before on the Marine's face had her shocked and unable to move.

"Run Sacha. Run!"

She slid to the rug, and she closed her eyes. She saw his face, heard him yell to her to run, then saw his injury. She cried harder. "Why? Why, damn it?"

She could hardly breathe she was hysterical as the whole experience came crashing back. The guns going off, her running for cover and shooting terrorists. Physically fighting her attackers off and then running for miles for days and selling what she had to survive and to live. She curled up in a ball and banged her fists on the rug until she could no longer move them.

She couldn't catch her breath, and when she felt the hand on her shoulder, she reacted in fear and surprise, only to wind up on her back on the floor with Toro holding her arms down by her sides so she would stop hitting him, straddling her hips.

"Easy, Sacha it's just me."

She didn't want to fight with him, with anyone. She closed her eyes, and she lay back on the rug. He lay over her, staring down at her face. He released her arms and caressed the tears from her cheeks.

"Nice easy breaths. Look at me and just breathe and know that you're safe here with all of us."

She locked onto his dark-blue eyes, seeing the worry, the strength there. He continued to caress her tears from her eyes and then caress her arms as he sat above her. The sight of his masculinity and the firmness of his jaw. The eyes of a killer, a fighter, a patriot, looked down upon her, and she knew he could empathize with her reaction and emotions. He'd experienced all of what she felt as a soldier, as a human, and that out-of-control feeling. If, for one moment, she thought otherwise, she would make him move and she would close herself up in her shell and remain guarded. She was so damn tired. Tired of all the sadness she felt and the not knowing what it would be like to connect with a man on that intimate level. To connect with Charro and his three team members.

She knew that Damien and Elwood were there, too. She sensed them, but she wouldn't look away from Toro or the security she found in his eyes or the beauty of his bare chest filled with muscles. He wiped away her tears, and then, as she calmed down and realized that she was not resisting his control and power over her and instead absorbing an attraction to the man, she looked away.

"I'm okay now," she said to him.

But she wasn't. Her pussy throbbed, her breasts swelled with need as she felt the attraction, the desire to be held by Toro, to get a glimpse into what it might have been like if Charro had survived, had lived to get here with her.

"Just take your time," Elwood said, and he and Damien came into view as they took a seat on the couch right by her.

Toro caressed her hair.

"It's normal to not want to face the fear, the memories of your experience."

"That doesn't make it easier, Toro. I don't want to revisit it."

"But maybe it will help?" he suggested.

"To see Charro die right next to me? To watch his fear as he told me to run and then watch as the bullet hit him in the head and him fall to the ground right there beside me? How can that help?" she asked, tears rolling down her cheeks. He clenched his teeth, and she saw his jaw cave in and his eyes darken.

"I'm sorry that it happened. That you were there and saw it. You two were close?" he asked.

She swallowed hard. "I trusted him with my life. He told me that he wanted to get out, that he wanted to explore the feelings we had." She looked away from him, and locked gazes with Damien. He was, watching her, staring down at her from the couch.

"I lied to you. I was trying to make it go away. You were right. Just as he told you about me, he told me about the three of you and wanting us to meet. I didn't want to admit that. I didn't want to read into why. I still don't know why."

Toro clutched her cheek and chin. "Maybe he thought you could learn to trust us, too."

She stared up into his dark-blue eyes. She absorbed the way his fingers felt caressing her lips and how his body felt covering hers halfway, and suddenly, she wanted more. She wanted to know what would have happened if she and Charro had gotten out of Kabul together. What would have occurred here with him, her, Toro,

Damien, and Elwood? But that scared her, to let her defenses down like that and trust so fully. How could she? She was in danger. They were because they were keeping her in hiding, and God only knew who would come to find her eventually. She had so much to do. She needed to seek revenge. To bring justice for Charro's murder and for her team's murder. But her hands were tied. She couldn't access anything she normally had access to. She looked at Toro's lips.

"You can trust us, like you trusted Charro."

"I don't think I can," she whispered weakly, not even believing her own words as Toro pressed closer.

He lay over her body, his one thigh pressed between her legs as he caressed one hand up her arm and held her gaze.

"I think you already do. I think you know exactly what Charro was hoping for in bringing you here to meet us. I understand now. I didn't before, but now, I do, too."

He pressed his lips to hers and kissed her.

* * * *

Everything hit Toro all at once. The way his heart ached with concern at seeing Sacha so sad, so distraught over Charro's death. To know that Charro had intended to bring her here to meet them and maybe engage in the relationship they all felt could bring them the happiness and the bond they yearned for but thought men like them could never deserve. When Damien said that Sacha told him Charro never mentioned them to her, he'd felt defeated, like a dream, a hope they had counted on had disappeared into thin air. Now that Sacha had admitted she lied and that Charro had told her about them, he knew this was their chance.

He explored her mouth as he covered her body with his. He felt her hands move along his body, and he rocked against her. He caressed his fingers through her hair, cupped her head, and explored her fully. She felt incredible, sexy, and he didn't have to be as lucky as Damien, to have already seen her naked, to know that she was perfect.

He slowly pulled from her lips and kissed her chin, her neck, and she tilted her head back, allowing him further access to her body. He reached under the light black tank top she wore with no bra and cupped her breast.

"Toro." She gasped, popping her eyes open as she covered his hand.

"Don't deny the attraction."

"I'm not. I…" She looked to the left where Damien and Elwood looked on, sitting forward on the couch.

Toro brushed his thumb along her cheek and jaw, bringing her back to look at him as he moved his hand from her breast.

"Look at me," he said to her, and she immediately did. She looked up at him with those gorgeous light green eyes and an expression of uncertainty yet arousal. She would be their lover, their mate. He just knew it.

"They want to kiss you, too. They want to know if Charro was right about you, about all of us together."

A tear fell from her eye. He wiped her eye with his thumb as he held her face between his hands. Her hands were locked over his.

"Don't cry, baby. Charro was part of us, just like you were part of Charro. He believed that there was something special about you and that perhaps you were the one to bring us all together and bind us fully as a family. I want to know if he was right, don't you?"

She looked at Damien and Elwood then back at him.

"Yes, I do. But is this right? I've put you in danger by remaining here, knowing that there must be people trying to find me," she whispered. He smiled and then released her cheeks and sat up. He stood and then reached out his hand.

"Come on. Let's sit down on the couch and talk. We have plenty of time and nowhere to run off to. We were meant to come find you. Charro, if he'd lived and was stuck in danger with you, would have called us in to come help. We know that for a fact. Let us get to know you, and you can get to know us."

She took his hand, and when he pulled her up, her breasts bounced in the tank top, and he felt his cock harden in his jeans. She would be their lover. He had no doubt in his mind. But what he did worry about was whether, after such an ordeal in the field, she would be able to open up her heart fully, or would she keep running out of fear and remain under cover? It was a chance he was willing to take, and all because of Charro.

* * * *

Damien rubbed his eyes. It was three a.m., and they were sitting in the game room on the couch surrounding Sacha. In the past two weeks, she'd avoided speaking with them for long periods of time. She'd been aggressive in her verbal responses and even combative at times, the strongest when Toro challenged her that day and accused her of potentially have PTSD.

She held strong, refusing to show weakness or admit to the fear and distrust she still had. But seeing her curled up in a ball on the rug, crying, tormented, pulled at his heart. Plus, she'd admitted that Charro had, in fact, mentioned them to her before. She was feeling the connection, the attraction between them, and Damien now wondered if Charro had been right. Was Sacha meant to be theirs?

She leaned against the couch. Toro kept her close, but she didn't reciprocate his caresses. They looked around at the pictures.

"When was that one taken?" she asked, pointing to a larger picture, an eleven-by-fourteen of the group of them at the Army game, tailgating.

"That was taken up at the West Point Academy game in New York. We met up with a bunch of our buddies. Charro has a cousin, Seno, who works at the academy. He graduated from there and helps with the Black Nights, a parachuting team," Damien told her.

"Yeah, it's pretty cool stuff. They parachute down into parades, and at all the home games at the Army stadium," Elwood added, looking at the picture and seeming serious.

Damien felt his chest tighten. He hated this shit. He hated having to remember the good times and be sad because the person they remembered was dead, killed in battle. It sucked.

He leaned forward and ran his fingers through his hair then rubbed his neck.

"I didn't know he had a cousin. Did he have other family?" she asked, wringing her fingers together , eyes filling with tears and appearing saddened at that fact. He wondered if she and Charro had been lovers and why he hadn't told her about his cousin, aunt, and uncle.

"His cousin, aunt, and uncle are all he has. He had a tough life. Didn't he tell you?" Elwood asked.

She looked at him and shook her head. "We talked about regular things."

"But you were intimate, weren't you?" Toro asked.

She shook her head, and her eyes welled up with ears. "Never. He hadn't even told me that he wanted me to spend our time off together, and to meet the three of you, until that day. A few minutes before he died."

"Damn," Elwood said and looked at Damien.

Damien looked at her. At her toned arms and her abundant breasts pouring from the tank top, which she tried unsuccessfully hiding from their view with a small pillow. They already knew she wasn't wearing a bra. Hell, he already knew what she looked like naked.

He swallowed hard.

"What did he tell you about me?" she asked.

Toro looked at Elwood and Damien.

Damien stared into her gorgeous green eyes. "He had a lot of nice things to say about you. How smart you are, how beautiful and strong."

"He said you were one tough Marine, and he worried about you," Elwood said.

"Worried about me?"

"Yeah, he said he was getting worried, too. That things were changing too fast and he didn't think he wanted to stay in the middle of the heat anymore. He said he wanted to bring you here," Damien told her.

She held his gaze as Damien sat next to her. He looked away, wanting and feeling so much. Was it just a crazy idea that Charro had planted in their heads about sharing Sacha and making her their woman? If so, then why was he feeling more and more connected to her as each day passed? Why now was he feeling protective and possessive of her?

He felt her hand on his back, rubbing it. Then she leaned forward and hugged his arm. "I'm sorry. This has to be so hard for you guys, too, to talk about Charro and to remember things he said."

Damien turned his head to look at her, their lips close, her head nearly against his. He looked into her light sage green eyes and felt so much.

"It's hard for you, too. You saw him die, but he did it doing something he loved, and that was fighting for this country of ours and protecting you. I guess it feels better to talk about it, about him, and remember the good times. To know what he thought about you and share it with you and this idea that we could all be together."

Her eyes widened, but she didn't pull away, not even right before his lips touched hers.

He turned into her, and she wrapped her arms around his shoulders and wound up on his lap, straddling his waist. He ran his hands along her thighs and up her arms to her head as he deepened the kiss. The attraction, the chemistry, was so intense, so different than anything he ever felt before.

She felt it, too. She had to as she squeezed her thighs tighter against him and kissed him back.

He wanted to feel more of Sacha, and he began to explore her body, run his hands back to her thighs, over the loose lounge pants she wore, and then up her ribs.

She gasped and pulled back. He forgot about her bruises.

"Oh fuck, I forgot. Jesus, baby, are you okay?" he asked her. She swallowed hard.

"I'm okay. That was…"

"Intense, wild, sexy as damn hell to fucking watch," Elwood said to her as he moved closer. He reached out and caressed her chin and then clutched it between his fingers before he started to lean forward.

Damien held his breath. He didn't know how she would react or if she would deny the feelings and push him away. But he felt relieved when she closed her eyes and tilted her chin in welcome to Elwood's kiss.

* * * *

Elwood had to kiss her, too. He couldn't just stand here and watch his brothers take her lips and explore her body with their hands and not participate. The attraction and connection in the room was palpable, and real, so real he felt it in every part of him, not just his cock. Sacha was sexy, beautiful, capable, and a soldier, a Marine like them. She did things to him, to his brothers, and made them feel things no one else had. How the hell had Charro known this would work? How had he found her and even begin to think of the possibilities?

He didn't even care as he explored her mouth and cupped her breast, rubbing his thumb along the hard little bud. She moaned into his mouth, reached up, and ran her hand along his shoulder and then the back of his neck. He loved the way it felt. He wanted more, but he sensed her pulling back, and he didn't want to scare her. In less than thirty minutes, three brothers she'd known only for the better part of two weeks had just made out with her.

* * * *

Sacha held on to Elwood's shoulders as she caught her breath. He stared into her eyes and licked his lower lip.

"I think Charro was onto something," he said to her, and she thought the same thing, yet feared so much. How could this work? Did she really want it to work? What would her father and her brother say? Did she even have a right to be here, to feel this good right now when her whole team had died in Kabul? That thought brought her mind back to where she needed to be. Where she was not so vulnerable to the need growing stronger in her heart and in her core.

"You have an untraceable phone line, correct?"

Elwood nodded at her and squinted his eyes at her instant change in subject.

"How about a secure computer and internet connection or maybe a scrambler we could attach to stop anyone from tracking our searches or anything coming in through the Internet?"

"What are you thinking, Sacha?" Damien asked. He moved up next to Elwood on the couch. She looked at Toro who was on the other side of Elwood. .

"I think we've waited long enough to look at the thumb drives."

Elwood reached up and caressed her cheek. "We're here to help you. Anything we can do to find the ones who killed Charro, we'll do."

She shook her head. "No, I can't ask you to do that, to get involved and risk your lives any further than you already have." She went to get up off his lap, but Elwood gripped her hips, stopping her.

"That's not your decision to make. It's ours."

"Charro was our family, we served together, and we will find the ones responsible for his death," Damien told her.

"I killed a lot of men that day, including the one who put a bullet in his head. This is different. This is going after a terrorist cell that has allies in people with access to our mission and plan down to the times we were to meet and get into position. Do you realize what that means?" she asked Damien.

"Yes, it means someone in our own government is helping these terrorist assholes," Damien said to her.

"We live to hunt down terrorist assholes, baby. You're not doing this alone," Toro said to her, and she nodded. But deep down she knew she'd made a promise that she wouldn't let them put their lives on the line. She'd lost Charro. She couldn't lose these three men who could potentially be her future and were the only lasting memory of Charro she had left.

"Let's get some rest, and we'll begin in a few hours," Damien said to her. He stood up, reached over, and cupped her cheek. She tilted her chin up toward him, and he leaned down and kissed her lips then ran his thumb along her lower lip.

Suddenly she fought between giving into the desire to go to bed alone and take her time getting to know these men or throwing inhibition to the wind and taking them to bed with her. One glance at Damien's muscles and sexy macho demeanor and she was leaning toward the latter.

"I'll walk you to bed," Toro said to her as she rose up off Elwood's lap and felt his hands linger against her hips.

When Toro took her hand, she looked up into his eyes, feeling aroused once again by the difference in height and how large and muscular he was. She looked at Elwood and Damien and gave a soft smile as Toro led her from the living room.

* * * *

Elwood leaned back in the chair and exhaled. Damien was straight faced as he took the seat next to him.

"Damn, she's fucking incredible," Elwood said, and Damien exhaled, too, as he looked around at the pictures.

They were all fond, fun memories of good times and a lasting friendship. They'd spent so many years fighting for their country then trying to maintain some form of normalcy when they returned from all the heavy shit and sometimes near death experiences.

"You agree, don't you?" Elwood asked him.

He glanced at him and then looked straight ahead.

"I agree. She's the whole package then some."

"But?"

"She's young, man. I'm thirty-six fucking years old, and she's twenty-six. I'm slowly weaning my way out of the military and doing dangerous shit. The three of us have been. She doesn't seem like she wants to be finished. Like she's thinking that once she finds the ones responsible for her team's murders that she'll stop, and even that could take forever. She may never find them."

"She'll find them because we're going to help her. I know it all seems so crazy. Meeting her like this, knowing what Charro hoped for and knowing that he doesn't get to experience this with Sacha as he planned. But I have this crazy feeling that it's going to work. It's going to take time, Damien. But I think the three of us are more than ready to put in that time, give her that patience, and see where this leads."

"And if she decides that she isn't ready, that she wants to go back inside as an operative, then what? Are you ready to kiss her good-bye and say see you whenever and then worry day and night? Imagine the bad shit we know these fucking individuals are capable of. Imagine them capturing her, striking her, raping her then putting a bullet in her head." Damien ran his fingers through his hair.

"No. I'm not going to think about those things because I asked you guys, and my loved ones, to not think of the bad things that could happen and all the terrible stuff that could go wrong. I asked for prayers, for protection, and for them, for you guys, to be here for me upon my return to say it's over and everything is going to be all right.

As soldiers, as mates to a woman Marine in active duty, we'll have to learn to do the same."

Damien looked at him. "I don't know if I can, and we haven't even had sex with her yet."

"You have a point. Maybe it won't be easy, but sometimes you have to suck up your own fears and insecurities in order to support someone you care about. Let's see what happens. Maybe we'll get lucky and those thumb drives and microchips will have a list of names and all we'll need to do is find someone in the government we can trust to take care of business."

"I already have someone in mind." Elwood looked at him strangely.

"Who?"

"Sparrow."

He saw his brother's eyes darken and squint. He shouldn't be surprised. Sparrow was their number one secret weapon of operations. He was more than an asset, a lifesaver, a capable, reliable, and resourceful friend. He was a spy, a man of a thousand faces, identities, and capabilities, and he could make anything happen. He could even make someone disappear, figuratively and literally.

"We haven't seen or heard from him or his brothers in months."

"That doesn't mean we can't get in contact with him. Let's not even talk about it. Maybe, like you said, we'll get lucky."

"Yeah, maybe."

* * * *

Toro couldn't resist touching Sacha. They stood by the doorway to her bedroom, just staring at one another and not moving. He reached out and ran his hand over her shoulder under her hair to her head. She tilted up toward him as he leaned down to kiss her. When their lips touched, it was perfect. It felt perfect, especially as she ran her hands up against his bare chest and kissed him back. That kiss grew deeper, and he ran his other hand along her hip to her ass and squeezed her to him. The flimsy pajama pants couldn't hide the heat of her sex as he pressed fingers lower over the crack of her ass to her pussy. She pulled from his mouth.

"Stay with me," she whispered, and he was shocked as he squinted at her.

"Not to have sex but to hold me and stay with me in bed. Can you?" she asked him. He didn't think twice as he pulled her into the room and then stood by the bed.

"Get in and I'll turn off the lights."

She climbed up onto the mattress, her ass sticking out and wiggling as she crawled up the bed from the bottom. He walked to the other side, tuned off the lamp, and climbed into bed under the covers.

He moved right in next to her and pulled her close. She turned in his arms and pressed her ass and back against him. His cock hardened as he wrapped one arm around her waist and the other above the pillow and her head. He leaned over and kissed her temple.

"Close your eyes and sleep. I've got you."

His words made his heart pound and his cock beg to be deep inside of her, fucking her, claiming her as his woman. But she needed time. Tonight wasn't the right moment, no matter how hard his dick was.

She felt good against him, warm, muscular, and sexy. He inhaled her shampoo and then the scent of her body lotion. He couldn't help but to scatter kisses along her shoulder and neck as he snuggled closer in need of her scent, her warmth, like she needed his. It wasn't long before he heard her sleeping, and then he rested, too, hoping to get hours like this with Sacha in his arms.

Chapter 3

"We go ahead with our plans in three weeks. Both the senators and congressman will be there, and our investor wants them out of the picture," Mahem told his three main commanders.

"You're not worried about the thumb drives missing as well as the woman?" his commander Dawson asked him.

Mahem ran his hand along his jaw. "It doesn't matter. I lied about his name being on those thumb drives. There are intricate details about our team, but it won't matter once you detonate those bombs and kill Senators Roland and Campbell, as well as Congressman Lewis. They cannot make it to elections. They are a threat, and as far as our investor is concerned, he wants them eliminated so they can't run."

"Why not just expose their criminal activity and personal investments in the arms deals they're involved in? That would get them out of running for office," Valan, another commander, asked.

"Well, it seems these three have really pissed them off. It's also an opportunity for Black Out, our organization, to gain some respect and media coverage. We're a small organization, but once we blow this crap out of that stadium and kill those politicians, everyone will know the name Black Out."

"Okay, we'll get everyone trained and ready to leave for the States. We have our connections in New York. There's a place we can hole up until the time. Valan and Hazeil are taking care of infiltrating the stadium and getting things planted ahead of time. It will be a piece of cake," Dawson told Mahem. Mahem smiled and nodded at his three commanders.

"Good, get things started. I'll keep on top of any sightings of the female Marine, but I doubt she is alive. Marine or not, from the pictures I've seen of her, she wouldn't have lasted long out in the desert or on the streets. With a body like hers, if she lived, she's someone's bitch right now and being used as the American whore she is. My only regret with that is that I couldn't kill her myself after she took the lives of my cousins and my brother."

"If she is alive and we find out, we will bring her to you so you can finish her off, Mahem," Dawson told him then bowed his head before he and the others left the room.

Mahem looked down at the small pictures of his family, of his two cousins and brother as they trained in the camps. She'd killed more than twelve men on her own. If she was alive and he found out, he would do everything in his power to have her killed. Even if it meant returning to the United States, a country he turned his back on a decade ago.

* * * *

Toro awoke, hearing the screams and feeling Sacha's body shake against his. He snapped out of his sleep. The morning sun filtered through the shades and cast light over both of them. She was crying, moaning, and he caressed her side and her arms as she screamed.

"What's going on?" Damien asked, running into the room with his gun drawn, wearing only boxers. Elwood followed, looking the same.

She cried out and sat upward, her eyes locking on the men, their guns, and she panicked. Toro had a feeling she was still lost in her nightmare as she cried out, "No." Then he straddled her body, laying over her.

"Calm down, Sacha, you're okay. They heard you screaming, and they came in with guns to protect you."

Her red-rimmed, glistening eyes locked onto his. She stared at him as if processing the situation, and then she wrapped her arms around his neck and kissed him.

That kiss grew deep and wild in no time. He let her roll him to his back as their lips parted, and she sat above him, straddling his waist.

"Help me forget. Help me, Toro." She lifted the hem of her tank top up over her head and tossed it to the side.

He cupped her breasts, feeling how large and firm they were as he held her gaze.

"Are you sure, Sacha?" he asked her.

"Yes. Please. I want you. I want to. I'm safe." She leaned down closer. He suckled her breast into his mouth and tugged on her nipple. Behind her, the bed dipped, and he saw Damien lean over her and kiss her neck.

"Sacha?" Damien said her name, and she looked at him.

"Please, Damien, Elwood, I want this. I need this, to feel connected, lost in your bodies and in your embraces. Please make love to me." The tears spilled from her eyes, and Toro cupped her cheek and wiped them away.

"We want you, too. This is right. We need this as well," he told her, and she leaned down to kiss his lips, and he rolled her to her back.

He sat up, and he cupped her breasts.

"You're so damn beautiful," Toro said to her, and then he lifted up, stood at the edge of the bed, and shoved his boxers off.

Her eyes widened as she took in the sight of his cock and he hoped she was impressed. He reached for her pajama pants and pulled them down. She watched as his eyes absorbed her bruised skin and injuries first then her luscious breasts before her well-shaven pussy. He licked his lips.

"Damn, woman, you're wet and ready."

He spread her thighs and lowered between them, licking her cunt and shoving his tongue into her deeply.

She grabbed his hair, tilted her head back, and moaned as he ate at her cream. He felt the bed dip on either side of her, and one glance upward and he saw his brothers. They were feasting on her breasts, raising her arms above her head.

"Oh God, Toro. Toro, what are you doing?" she asked as he stroked his tongue from pussy to anus back and forth.

"Getting you ready."

"I'm more than ready. Oh!" She gasped.

Damien and Elwood tugged hard on her nipples.

"You're gorgeous, baby. Your body is perfect," Damien told her and then leaned up and kissed her deeply. She moaned and tilted her hips upward.

Toro pulled his mouth from her cunt and then pressed a finger up into her. She gasped and thrust, and he stroked in and out of her pussy before wiping the cream over her anus.

"Oh!" she cried out and exploded just as he pressed a wet digit over her lubricated anus. He slid his finger in, and she continued to shake from her orgasm.

"Holy shit, I think Sacha likes a finger in her ass," Elwood said.

"And one in her wet pussy," Damien said.

"Please, please, Toro." She begged for his cock, and it fed Toro's ego.

"I'm coming in, sweetness. Just exploring this body and what's mine."

He pulled his fingers from her cunt and then aligned his cock with her pussy.

"Here I come, honey. Relax those muscles and let me in."

He felt her tense and then relax as soon as the tip of his cock began to penetrate her pussy.

He nudged in over and over until he was inching deeper and deeper.

"Toro! Toro," she exclaimed, and he shoved all the way into her as his brothers released her arms and she hugged him tight.

He began to rock his hips as he kissed her forehead, her nose, and then her lips again. She ran her fingers along his back muscles and then to his shoulders while counter thrusting against him.

He stroked faster, deeper, trying to ease this itch deep within him.

The bed creaked and moaned, and she kissed him. She kissed his neck and suckled hard as he stroked into her pussy, trying to find his release. She countered, and he felt the gush of cream right before his cock grew extra thick and he came. He kissed her some more, and they hugged then rolled to the side, his hand caressing her ass cheek as they calmed their breathing and recovered together.

* * * *

Sacha was on fire. She'd never felt so connected to a man during sex before. Although her experiences were limited, she still felt how different this was, especially now as Toro kissed her cheeks and then released her to Elwood.

She locked gazes with his big dark-blue eyes as he pulled her up into his arms and rolled to his back. She straddled his hips, and she ran her hands up and down his chest as he cupped her breasts.

"I love your body, Sacha. You're in perfect physical condition."

"I love your body, too, Elwood. All these muscles and this one." She ran her hand along his pectoral muscles then down his tight abs, before gripping his long, thick cock and stroking it as she raised upward.

He held her gaze. "Ride me, Sacha. Make me yours."

It sounded like an order, and she took it as one. She slowly sank down on his thick, hard cock. She had to ease her pussy over it and lift then sink, lift then sink until finally he was all the way in. She moaned, and so did he, and she felt him cup her breasts as she popped her eyes open to look at him.

Elwood was super sexy, just like his brothers. He had large, wide shoulders, tan skin, dark-blue eyes, and an expression of seriousness and control. She loved that. She was turned on by each of their dominant personalities, especially right now as Elwood began to thrust into her as he held her hips and spread her thighs wide. It seemed he had an itch to scratch, and he was making her moan with pleasure once again.

In and out, he stroked her cunt as he played with her breasts. She countered and then gasped as she felt the second set of hands on her hips from behind. She knew it was Damien, and her head began to spin with the idea of making love to more than one man at the same time.

She shivered as Damien's finger stroked over her anus and began to push into her ass. The slick nectar from her pussy lubricated her anus, and he began to counter Elwood's thrusts.

"Oh, Damien, Oh God, that feels so strange."

"But real good, baby, right?" Toro asked as he reached up and caressed her hair.

"I never did that before," she admitted as Elwood fucked her faster.

"Never? Damn, that's so sweet. We're going to take you together one day real soon. As soon as we get this ass ready for cock," Damien told her and stroked a finger faster into her ass.

She felt the fingers press over her pussy and spread her pussy lips as Elwood fucked her. Round and round, Toro manipulated her clit, sending tiny vibrations of need into her cunt. She creamed some more as she tilted her head back and moaned.

"You taste so sweet, baby. Taste yourself," Toro told her, and then she felt his thumb against her lips.

She parted them, and he pressed his finger into her mouth, and she tasted her cream. The combination of the feeling of never doing anything so brazen, along with the fact that Toro did this to her, had her screaming out another release.

"Oh hell yeah. Here I come," Elwood said and held her hips and thrust upward, keeping his cock buried deep to her womb.

He shook and she shivered then she felt the mouth against her neck and shoulder.

"My turn, baby. To make you mine," Damien whispered.

She felt his mouth suckle against her skin, and he nibbled her shoulder in a sensitive spot that had her panting for more. His arm wrapped around her waist, and he eased her back.

"Oh God."

She moaned and wondered if he were going to fuck her ass. Suddenly the idea appealed to her. But instead, the moment he lifted her up, Elwood eased out of the way, as did Toro, and Damien placed her on all fours on the bed. He spread her pussy and thrust right into her cunt from behind. She gasped, almost shocked at how thick and hard his cock was and how he didn't hesitate but, instead, took what he wanted. He was the commander, the leader, the man in control, and she loved it. It aroused her as she counter thrust back. He gripped her hips bones and began a series of fast, hard strokes.

"You feel so fucking good. You're so tight, baby. I won't last. Not with this sexy body and your tits rocking and swaying."

He eased his hands under her, over her belly, and up to her breasts. He cupped them with those masculine, large, warm hands of his, and she shivered as she came again.

She looked at Toro and Elwood. Elwood was washing his cock with a wet towel, and Toro was watching her and stroking his cock. Did he want to take her again, so soon?

"Here I come, baby. Here I come."

Damien held his cock in her cunt as he came. He shook and held her tight, and she closed her eyes and relished the sensation of being fucked by three men. He slowly pulled out of her, and she went to move, but Toro had other plans.

"Not yet. I need more." He took Damien's place, came in behind her, and eased his cock against her pussy. He ran the tip back and forth over her pussy then her anus. She shivered with anticipation.

"Such a nice tight ass. I can't wait to fuck it while Damien fucks that pussy and Elwood fucks your mouth."

He eased his hand over her shoulder and tilted her head to the side as he stroked into her pussy from behind. She felt stretched, awkward in this position, yet entirely turned on by his control. He brought his face closer to hers.

"Would you like to suck Elwood's cock?" he asked and then licked her lower lip.

"Yes," she said, and he kissed her, plunging his tongue in deeply as he increased the depths of his strokes into her pussy from behind.

Elwood crawled up onto the bed. She looked down at his cock, long, thick, with pre cum dripping from the tip.

"Suck him," Toro ordered.

She opened her mouth and took him in. He stroked her hair and held her head as she sucked up and down, bobbing her head. Behind her, Toro fucked her pussy faster, and then she felt his finger ease into her ass. It didn't burn so much this time, and as he thrust and fucked her while she fucked Elwood's cock, Toro stretched her anus, scissored his fingers, and added a second digit as he stroked. She couldn't take it and was losing focus.

"Fuck I'm there. I'm fucking there," Elwood said and shot his seed down her throat.

"Fuck," Toro cried out and pulled his finger from her ass and began to stroke deeper, faster into her cunt. She cried out and panted as Toro came inside of her pussy.

As he eased out of her pussy, she fell to the bed and tried catching her breath. Hands massaged her back and her ass, and then she felt the kisses.

"Shower, you and me, now," Damien said.

She blinked her eyes open at him and saw that fierce, controlled expression. Like a good soldier, she eased up, and before she could try to climb off the bed, Damien lifted her up into his arms. He kissed her mouth and then carried her to the bathroom. He set her feet down.

"You're incredible, Sacha. So fucking perfect."

He started the shower, and she stood there taking in the sight of Damien. He had a bit of scruff along his cheeks and upper lip. It added to his sex appeal and the macho roughness of his demeanor. His dark-blue eyes held hers as he eased his arm around her waist and hoisted her close against his muscled, chiseled chest. She gasped when his palm landed over her ass.

"When we make love to you together, it's going to be incredible. You'll be ours fully and in every way, and we'll be yours. This is just the beginning."

He was so serious, and his words, the meaning behind them, assaulted her senses. She wanted that, craved that, but it also scared her. She didn't know if she could open her heart and soul to them. The fear of what they did for a living, just like what she did, could stand in the way of letting herself go. But she didn't have time to process that as Damien lifted her up and brought her into the shower. He pressed her against the wall as she straddled his waist and the water fell upon them. Tilting her head back, he suckled her chin and kissed her lips then suckled her chin again. She felt his cock tap against her folds, and somehow she wanted him inside of her again. It was where life was perfect, and it didn't involve thinking or being scared. It was freedom. She rocked her hips against him, and he lifted her higher so he could suckle her breast. She reached between them and stroked his cock. He let go of her nipple as he tugged.

"Fuck, you got me so hard." He lowered her down over his shaft and began to sink into her depths. She pressed down, wanting, needing, that connection. It was overwhelming, and as they locked gazes, it all became so raw and real.

"Mine. All fucking mine." He practically growled as he covered her mouth and thrust into her deeply.

She kissed him, and it was wild. It became a challenge of control and power, but she gave in as he thrust so hard, so deeply into her cunt that she lost her breath and cried out her release. He continued to assault her senses and fuck her so hard, so fast that she didn't know where his desire and stamina came from, and then he grunted as he came, spreading her ass cheeks and pressing his cock to her womb as he shoved her hard against the wall and grunted. She hugged him tight, loving the feeling of being one with Damien, just like she had been with Elwood and Toro. It was crazy, and as he eased his cock from her pussy, she instantly thought of Elwood and Toro and making love to them again.

* * * *

It was proving to be difficult to keep their hands off of Sacha. Even now, after they'd all showered after making love all morning, Damien noticed that none of them seemed to be able to stay too far from her. After they grabbed some lunch, they headed to the office in the basement. Elwood held her hand as she held the envelope containing the only possible evidence and clue as to who had set her team up and killed them. It hadn't sat right with him before making love to Sacha, and it certainly felt worse now. He was instantly protective and possessive of her. Making love to her together with his brothers was magical and not something to take lightly. None of them were, but he couldn't shake the feeling that, once they were out of bed, she was a different person and back to business. Back to being tough and trying to prepare herself for what they would find on the thumb drives. He just hoped that was all holding her back and that she wasn't unable to commit to them on an intimate level.

Elwood sat down in front of the computer. He checked and rechecked the wires and all the software they had installed specially. It was safe and secure. No one could trace anything they did or looked at, and even if there was a tracking device on the thumb drives or microchips, it shouldn't matter. They had a scrambler that would redirect the signal elsewhere. But Damien was still a little nervous because technology changed on a daily basis, and anything was possible.

Damien took the other seat, and Toro held Sacha around the waist as he leaned against the other desk. His hand was splayed over her belly and hip and the low-rise light pants she wore. The midriff, long-sleeved shirt accentuated her toned belly and showed bits of the bruising on her ribs that he didn't like seeing on her. He hoped they healed quickly.

They looked at her, and she glanced at Toro, his expression firm as he released her and crossed his arms in front of his chest. She stepped between Elwood and Damien and opened up the envelope. She slid the contents onto the table.

"Okay, let's see what we have." Elwood lifted up the first gray and silver thumb drive. "It's not labeled."

"Either is the other one or the microchips, which we'll need a reader for," she said to him.

"We have that, too. It slides right into one of these," Damien told her as he showed her the small device.

Elwood went to put the thumb drive into the computer to read it.

She touched his arm. "Before we look at this, I need to ask you one more time. Are you guys sure you want in? Are you certain you want to be part of this? Because I can't guarantee your safety. Anything could happen. You know that?" she asked them.

Damien took her hand and brought it to his lips. "Trust us. We're doing this for you, for Charro, and for the good of what's right and for every soldier out there who has lost their life because of these people."

She nodded.

Elwood gave her a wink. "We're in this together. Let's see what we find."

Damien didn't understand any of the things he saw on the computer screen, but Sacha did. She started to decode the information, translating the language to English and then filtering through the contents.

"Sounds like they're planning an attack or a hit," Toro said to them.

Sacha continued to read what it said, and then she stopped. She covered her mouth with her hand. "This is a hit all right. It's for one in the States."

"What?" Damien asked, sitting forward in his seat. "Scroll down, Elwood. See what it lists there. Those numbers are a code. My team and I were able to track these codes and numbers and come up with a system Black Out used to communicate with one another. These numbers and letters are for the U.S. government. There's some sort of hit on U.S. soil."

"Shit. How the fuck do we figure out who, when, and where?" Toro asked, standing behind her. Sacha took the seat between Elwood and Damien.

"There's nothing else on this thumb drive," Elwood said.

"Put in the other one," Toro said from over her shoulder.

Damien handed it to Elwood, and the second the information pulled up onto the screen they were shocked.

It gave the date, who was going to be taken out, and a list of names of individuals doing the hit.

"Holy shit. We have our work cut out for us. We need to find out who these people are and what they look like," Elwood said as he started to type on the keyboard.

"We need to check out where these two senators and the congressman plan on being on that date." Toro moved along to another desk and computer.

"Wait. Are all these computers safe and guarded?" she asked.

"Yes," the three of them said at once, and they started to work.

Damien pulled out the microchip reader. As the info came up on the screen, he felt disappointed. "It'' a dud. There's nothing on there."

"Wait." She looked at the screen, and he didn't know what she was thinking. Then she typed some words onto the keyboard, and a password label came up. She pulled her lower lip between her teeth. "Damn, Anya, please tell me our guy coded this with the password we all know."

"Who is Anya?" he asked.

"Another agent who went missing the same day our mission turned to shit. Spence, our team leader, had a suspicion that she was taken out and her identity compromised. It was why I had to go in."

"What does she have to do with this password?" he asked.

"Well, our intel, the one who worked undercover in Black Out, was able to copy these thumb drives and file and then place them into this safe. But then we believe his identity was revealed and they killed him. At least that is what Spence felt happened. He said something about others interested in the thumb drives, but nothing more. As we caught wind of his death, we were trying to pull off this last part of the plan. He was to disappear for the night, and his cover would be fine. We would go in, open the safe, and take the thumb drives he copied. Except Anya never made it. She was killed, and I was forced to meet up with Charro and help him. But Charro never showed. I got worried, and I knew time was limited because Black Out's soldiers were closing in. I got into the office, got the thumb drives, and was about to leave when these guys came in with Charro and were beating the crap out of him. It was an intense moment."

"You killed them?" Toro asked her.

"Two out of three. Charro broke the third guy's neck. You know the rest."

"Well, put in the password so we can get the names and you can see if this Anya and the agent were legit."

She typed it in, and nothing happened. She typed it in again, and an alert popped up onto the screen.

"Fuck, it's protected," Damien told her.

"Protected? From whom? These were meant to be taken by us so we could close in on Black Out and take them down. It has to work." She typed in the password again and again. Damien covered her hand.

"Sacha, it isn't working. It was bullshit. This Anya and the agent working for you were probably double agents."

"No. No. Over ten people died that day on my team. We were not set up by Anya and the agent. No, it can't be true. That would mean it was all bullshit, a show, and that they killed us all for—"

She stood up, shoving the chair back as she turned around and stared at the wall with her fists by her side. She was fuming and trying to catch her breath. He felt terribly for her and angry as well. They were far greater casualties than what she had been told.

"Sacha?" Elwood said her name as She heard Toro stand up. She turned around and faced them.

"They're not getting away with this. They killed Charro and my entire team, for what? A decoy? A game of power to show that they knew there were undercover agents? No. No fucking way am I letting them get away with this. No way." She stared at the screen and the words indicating her password didn't work.

Damien pulled her onto his lap and hugged her. "We'll figure it out Sacha. We'll get them."

* * * *

"We got a hit. The tracking mechanism worked. Someone just opened up the microchip," Falcon called to his commander as they sat in the control room at headquarters. They had a secret base containing everything they needed to run their team's investigation. As Special Operatives, they worked privately on investigations involving terrorists and other crimes against the U.S. government. They had been hunting Black Out and its leader for months now. Charro was working as a double agent, but unfortunately his cover was blown. He was unable to make it out alive. They got there too late to help him.

"Jesus, who the fuck is it? Is it someone from Black Out? Mahem maybe?" Commander Chordero asked.

"No, sir, this isn't coming from the Middle East. It's coming from New York."

"What?" Chordero asked and rushed over to take a look at the monitor and the tracking mechanism.

"The signal was a flash hit. The computer automatically records the findings but doesn't quite pinpoint the exact location," Falcon told him.

"What the hell is going on? Does this mean these fuckers are here, in the States, and getting ready for something?" Axel asked as he joined them.

"I don't know what it means. The only reason we even got wind of there being a copy of the thumb drive and microchip was that brief chatter our intelligence on the inside picked up on," Chordero said to them.

"Don't remind me about that. We were thirty minutes late to the party and don't have a soul to interrogate for answers," Falcon said.

"Yeah, just a bunch of dead bodies. Where's that list you uncovered while breaking into those government files, Falcon? The female Marine that wasn't accounted for, where did she come from? Where does she live? I want everything you've got on her."

"Chordero, you seriously think she's the one who took out all those men from Black Out, then escaped from Kabul by herself, then got into the United States and is in New York with those thumb drives?"

"I've seen stranger things, Falcon. Our double agent placed those thumb drives in that safe for either us or those government operatives to find. Charro knew what needed to be done, and I'm still wondering how he didn't get those thumb drives himself and get them to the drop-off location to meet you and Axel there," Chordero said to them.

"Unless he handed them off to this Marine for some reason and she got out alive," Falcon said.

"No, something went terribly wrong. Someone was working against them and against us. This double layer of protection, having our team ensure delivery of those thumb drives, was intervened by someone inside. There's no other explanation. Commander Maddox thinks so, too. We need to find out where those thumb drives are so we can get those codes and you, Falcon, can unscramble them, decode them, or whatever needs to be done before Black Out succeeds in whatever the fuck they are planning. Find them for us. Now."

Falcon nodded and continued to work on the computer while the rest of them found out more about the one female Marine unaccounted for.

Chapter 4

"I want to know what the fuck is going on?" Senator Dupree spoke into his cell phone as he stood by the window in his office. He had a bad feeling in his gut. Too much was riding on these fucking rogue Marines. He was getting too old for this shit. It was going to be his last stint as a senator if he could ensure that asshole Senator Jay Roland didn't get elected in the upcoming election. Eliminating his cohorts, Congressman R.R. Lewis and Senator Lilly Campbell, would be an added security as well. What the fuck was Mayhem and his team doing?

"We have everything under control. The plan is in motion, and we should be in the States within the next few weeks as planned," Mahem told him.

"What about those thumb drives, the Marine that's unaccounted for? What's going on?" he asked.

"We're working on it now. We believe she may have escaped to the States."

"To the United States? What the fuck? Who is this woman? What's the name?"

"We're taking care of it, Dupree. Don't you worry, I'm going to personally make sure she pays for the aggravation she's caused me."

"The name?" he pushed, raising his voice.

"Sacha Smith."

It took a moment for Dupree to process her name. Then it hit him. It couldn't be. There was no way that Sacha was Devan Smith's daughter. How fucking crazy would that be? Her Marine father was one of the main reasons why Dupree almost got busted in connection to some arms deals in Africa. He even tried to get some of their people to eliminate Devan Smith when he and his team of soldiers overtook a military camp and confiscated all the guns and ammo. It was a fucking mess and had cost Dupree millions.

"Are you still there?" Mahem asked.

"Yes. I am. I know this woman's family."

"What?"

"Yes, I know the father. He was a Marine, recently retired, and not because he wanted to retire." Dupree smirked. He thought that was enough to get rid of Smith. His pull on the inside with a few higher-ups had Smith removed for being too intense in his training for the troops and too "old school," as a lot of the old-timers referred to him. He was tough, and with a commander like Smith, there would be no room to persuade soldiers to look the other way and grease their palms on missions. Men like Smith fucked up all of Dupree's dirty deals. Good riddance to, the fucking psycho Marine.

"So his daughter is going to continue to be a problem?" Mahem asked.

"Seems like the apple doesn't fall far from the tree. There's a son, too. He's also a Marine. I'll find out where he is. We may need a little advantage when the time comes."

"You want to grab the brother then use him to stop the sister from interfering in this?"

"I was thinking that could work, and then we can take out all three of them, the old man included."

"You can take him out now. I've got men in position in the States already."

Dupree thought about that a moment. "As much as I would like to say yes to that, I don't think it would be a wise move. Too many questions would be asked and red flags raised, especially when the daughter is missing and the son suddenly disappears from wherever he is. I'll take care of the brother and the father. You find the sister, and fast, or we will have to smoke her out. I want this wrapped up nice and neat with a big red bow on top. You understand me, Mahem? I don't need any close calls, and I certainly don't need to get caught."

"It will work out just fine. Keep me posted, and I'll let you know when I find her and when my team and I will be heading to New York."

Dupree disconnected the call and then exhaled. He remembered years back when he was a young congressman learning the ropes and how to take advantage of his power and to manipulate the system. The access he had to such crucial military operations was vital in making the money he made. Devan Smith had nearly caught him red-handed. The son of a bitch always suspected him of being involved but had no concrete evidence, and his accusations had been used against Smith in the long run. He was reprimanded by his officials for accusing Dupree of criminal activity, and the dick never let him forget it. Dupree squinted and felt the anger for the man resurface. It was instant. That hatred, annoyance, and need for revenge. This could finally set Smith in his place and make him realize that the Marines, the patriot he was, would never overpower men like Dupree, given their capabilities. There were just more bad guys than good guys, and the sap was too stupid to join in and live life rich and comfortably.

Men like Smith believed in the United States Constitution, the Rambo-Dirty Harry days of good guys prevailing. That wasn't the case anymore. There were double agents, double-dealings, people's lives exchanged for guns, money, drugs, and power.

He smirked and chuckled then walked over to the small mini bar in his office. He poured himself a small snifter of brandy, an expensive one, which only his connections and successes afforded him to have. Another of many the pluses to working the system.

How ironic that Devan's daughter was at the center of this fuckup. He thought about that a moment. He wondered what she looked like, what her credentials were, and how the fuck she's taken out so many men. A woman, no less. But Devan had probably helped to train her himself. She couldn't be underestimated, like he had nearly underestimated her father and could have lost everything.

He swallowed down the rest of the brandy and then felt the heat move down his throat to his belly. Devan and Sacha were thorns in his side and in this mission. The brother would be a good tool to use as bait to coax them out and get them to cooperate. Then he would issue the order to kill the three of them.

He smiled.

"The Smiths won't be a problem for me ever again."

* * * *

Sacha stood by the big window looking over the back porch. She had her hand on the door and debated about walking outside. It was cold out. She hadn't grabbed a sweater, but she felt so hot, so angry and confused. None of this situation made sense. She started to wonder what had happened to Anya. Why would the password change? They all needed to know the password in order to process the thumb drives, and Anya was the one who had a contact in Black Out's gang of military terrorists.

She had the small sensation of fear in her belly. She needed to think, to process this, and she couldn't be afraid that someone was out there in the woods watching her and waiting to take her out. The men said she was safe here, and she trusted them. That thought brought more concern. She was putting Damien, Elwood, and Toro at risk.

The fact that she feared getting some fresh air enraged her, too. She was angry, hot-headed right now, as she pulled the sliders opened and then closed it behind her. The cold air collided against her heated skin, and she welcomed it.

She stepped across the porch, got to the railing, and looked down the steep embankment underneath. It was a gorgeous cabin, set in a private setting in the woods. She listened to the sounds around her as she grabbed onto the railing, squeezed it tight, and processed the information and what she knew right now.

Someone from the inside had set them all up. Either that, or perhaps it was someone within the team. She went through each of the people's names and what their specific jobs were. When she came to Charro, her belly tightened. When she asked herself if he could have been working for Black Out, she forced herself to not answer quickly but instead to imagine if it were true and he had. But he'd been killed. Right next to her as they ran together. He could have asked her to give him the thumb drives, but he hadn't. He trusted her with him like an equal. There was no way he was involved. But then she thought about how he'd been late to get to the office and how he'd been detained by soldiers of Black Out. How did they know he was there? How did they know about the thumb drives and chips?

Anya?

Anya had access to all of it and was the main contact and connection in sending them in for those thumb drives. But she was a no-show. Had she been killed? Was she working for Black Out and remained with them and sent the team in there to be sacrificed? It was a good possibility. But then she thought about today and the tracking system attached to the thumb drives. Who'd placed them there? Could Black Out have known about the operation and set them all up? Set up Charro, Anya, and the others to coax them out? But how did they know about the copies unless they knew about Agent Teddy Riley who'd made copies of them? Shit. Who the fuck was working for who?

She lowered her head and gripped the railing. Who were the leaders of Black Out? Were they not even terrorists from another country at all? Were they rogue U.S. military hired out by someone to take out the two senators and one congressman? Could all the hype, the other hits throughout the Middle East, have been decoys to what they were really after and why they really were?

Shit.

She heard the door slide open then the heavy footsteps coming toward her. She knew it was one of the men, and she tightened up until she felt the large, heavy jacket drape over her shoulders.

"You'll get sick out here with no jacket, baby," Elwood told her as he wrapped her in the jacket. She put her arms through the sleeves, and he wrapped his arms around her. He pressed his chin onto her shoulder.

"Are you doing okay?" he asked.

"Honestly? No. I'm not. I'm frazzled, confused, angry, and I don't even know who in my team went rogue. That's what's pissing me off so much. Someone gave up our mission. A lot of undercover operatives died. Charro died, too."

"I know you're angry. I would be pissed, too. But you know what I would do?"

"What?" She turned around in his arms to face him. She looked up into his dark-blue eyes. He towered over her and was filled with muscles in the thick, heavy blue-checkered flannel he wore.

She leaned back against the railing and he pressed his hands on either side of her against it, caging her in as he held her gaze.

"I would go through every person who was part of the team and try to remember their role in this. Who would have had access to information? Who was in charge of communications, location, security, anything that processes through the scenario and how things went down."

"I was just doing that, and to be honest, it's difficult to stand here and imagine one of the team being rogue and working for the bad guys."

He caressed a strand of her long brownish-blonde hair behind her ear. He caressed her cheek.

"I know it is, but it could help you figure things out and process it all."

She thought about that a moment.

"Elwood, they were all good soldiers, good operatives who worked together for two years."

"Some have to stand out more than others with their capabilities as being the inside informant."

"Just Anya and Charro come to mind." She then winced as she saw his expression change, but then he looked away, took a deep breath, and released it.

"Okay, as uncomfortable as that may be, let's try to put our personal connections to Charro aside and process this. Could Charro have been working for Black Out? If so, why would the soldiers have stopped him from getting into the office and getting those thumb drives?"

"Because it was a setup to cover his role as an agent?" she suggested.

"Then why, after you took out the men and he and you escaped, did he allow you to maintain possession of the only evidence you and the team would have to prove your mission a success?"

"Because he was playing his role to the fullest and thought we would get out alive and then he could get the thumb drives from me and do what he had to do next."

"Kill you?" Elwood asked.

The tears filled her eyes, and she looked away.

He cupped her cheeks and held her gaze. "Never. He wanted you. He wanted the five of us to be together. There's no way he was going to kill you."

"If you're right, then the only other two people that could have been rogue were Anya and Spence."

"Spence? Who was he, and what was his role?" he asked rubbing her shoulders and her arms and then placed his hands on the railings on either side of her again.

She explained about him being a desk guy, seemingly nervous and unsure in confirming the meet-up locations and then changing them at the last second.

"Perhaps he had a feeling something was up with Anya and he thought she was rogue? If so, he wouldn't send you to the original meet-up location. He would change it as a precaution."

"And not tell me?"

"You were about to go into a hot situation. How would that add to your stress level?"

"That's a possibility. Do you think Damien and Toro have found out more about those senators and congressman yet?"

"We can go check. But first things first."

He cupped her chin and neck, tilting her head back as he held her gaze.

"You're strong, you're beautiful, and you're not alone in this. Remember that." He pressed his lips to hers and kissed her deeply.

Soon his hands were moving under the coat to her hips then under her shirt. His cool hands made her shiver, but the heat of her pussy and the way his body felt so hard and big against hers warmed her thoroughly. She kissed him back and ran her hands up his shoulders over the flannel and to his head. She stood up on tiptoes and kissed him back. She felt hot, wild with need, and pulled at his shirt and then shifted her hands down to his jeans. She undid the zipper, reached down, and gripped his cock. He moaned into her mouth and pinched her nipple, and she moaned back.

It was wild and uninhibited as he undid her pants next and pressed them down with his hands as their lips parted and their eyes locked.

"I want you, here, now."

"Yes."

He shoved her pants down and pressed a finger to her cunt. She grabbed onto his shoulders and gasped as she maintained her balance.

He stepped from one leg of his jeans and compression shorts. Then he pulled fingers from her cunt, and she stepped from one leg and he lifted her up and against him. Their bodies collided, she straddled his waist, and he pressed her against the siding of the house.

The cool air collided against her pussy, adding to the sexual stimulation. He stroked right into her, and they both moaned in relief. It was so carnal, so natural of a sensation. Like being one, connected like this healed everything and made it perfect. Nothing else mattered but his cock penetrating her cunt, stroking, fucking her with pleasure over and over again.

"Your hands feel so good. Oh God, Elwood, you're so thick and hard," she told him as he fucked her and caressed his hands up her back under the shirt and the coat she wore.

He stroked into her, faster, deeper, and she took in every sensation, sight, smell, and sound around them. His moans of pleasure, the scent of pine from the woods, the smell of the logs of the home against her back, his cologne, the feel of the hard wood against her back, and even harder sensation from the thrusts of his cock moving in and out of her pussy.

"Elwood, faster, harder."

She pushed him for more, and he covered her mouth and kissed her again as he continued to thrust into her. She ran her hands up under his shirt, and then he pulled from her mouth, gripped her hands and brought them above her head, and fucked her relentlessly. She locked gazes with his intense dark-blue eyes, and she knew she was falling in love with him. He was marking her as his woman. She felt it deep in her womb, as strong and apparent as a stain against her outer skin, but this was eternal, forever. The tears filled her eyes, and she closed them tight and came hard, shaking, convulsing on his cock as he followed, grunting, moaning, and thrusting until he held his cock deep in her cunt and came.

He released her arms and hugged her to him. "You're perfect, Sacha, and all mine forever."

* * * *

Franco Smith was relieved to be back on U.S. soil. His concern the entire time in Iraq was for his sister, Sacha. As he traveled through the airport and onto the main parking area, he wondered how she was holding up. He knew that the Vancouver men had her safe and secure. They'd gotten her out of India alive. It was going to be hell not seeing her. He was so worried, and he was trying so hard to not interfere in the situation. He reminded himself that it had to be worse for his father. His dad knew a lot of people and had a lot of connections. Allowing the Vancouver men to be her protectors took a lot. But his dad also knew what they were capable of. They could be the best protection anyone could provide for her.

The terrorist group, Black Out, was fierce. They were responsible for a multitude of terrorist hits throughout the Middle East. It wasn't until there was chatter from undercover operatives and agents that the U.S. government learned of Black Out's intention to bring those acts of violence and terror onto U.S. soil.

No one knew anything about the leaders and their followers, and that was why Sacha and her team had been sent into the mission two years prior. He wished he knew more details than that, but what he'd found out he'd pushed Commander Maddox to the limit for. He'd never felt so helpless in his life.

As he headed through the parking lot looking for his vehicle, he located it and hit the unlock button. It was late, midnight, as he opened the door then opened the side back door to put his duffel bag inside.

The sound of the click of a gun and then the feel of the hard metal pressed to his head was sudden. He froze. He let his guard down. Was it a mugger? But then he heard the Middle Eastern accent.

"If you move or resist, I have no qualms about putting a bullet in your head right here. Either way, we get what we want. Your sister."

He placed his hands palms down onto the car.

"Wise choice, soldier."

Franco clenched his teeth. He didn't know what to do, but as his hands were cuffed behind his back and he was led between vehicles over toward a van, he knew this was going to make matters worse. They would probably use him to bait Sacha. How could he have been so stupid? Sacha would put him first. *I fucked up.*

* * * *

"Isn't it a bit cold out here for that?" Damien asked standing by the sliders watching Elwood hug Sacha. The sight of them with their pants down and her bare legs wrapped around Elwood's naked lower half had his cock hard and ready to take her next.

She pulled her bottom lip between her teeth and appeared embarrassed.

"It was cold, and I needed to warm our woman up," Elwood said and kissed her nose before he eased out of her body. She lowered to her feet, one shoe on her right foot and one sock on the other foot. Her shoe sat with her jeans in a pile on the floor.

"What's up?" Toro asked, joining them.

Damien looked at Toro as he took in the sight. But then Sacha bent for her jeans, and Elwood pulled on his compression shorts. The sight of her bare ass aroused him.

"Stop, Sacha," Damien said to her, and it came out sounding like an order.

She stopped and turned around, holding the jacket around her body. It was Elwood's, and it was huge. It covered her bare pussy and ass, but her long, sexy legs were still in view.

"Elwood, grab her stuff and meet us upstairs." He stepped out and took her hand. The second he had her in the house, Toro took position behind her and began to remove her jacket. She shivered.

"Don't worry, sweetheart. We're going to warm you up really fast." Damien pulled her close and kissed her deeply. She wrapped her arms around his shoulders, and he ran his palms along her ass and squeezed her ass cheeks.

Elwood closed and locked the sliding door.

When Damien released her lips, he lifted her shirt up and over her head. Her breasts bounced in the bra she wore. He took that off next, and now she was completely naked except for the one sock and the sock and boot. Toro chuckled.

Damien lifted her up into his arms, and she straddled his waist, her breasts level with his mouth.

"Let me get this," Toro said and pulled off the boot.

Damien suckled her nipple and pulled on it. She ran her fingers through his hair and pressed his mouth snugger against her breast.

He moaned and suckled harder.

"Damien," she hissed.

"We need you, too." Toro cupped her cheek and kissed her mouth.

When Toro released her lips, Damien released her breast and looked at her. She looked so sexy and desirable.

"Upstairs to the bedroom," he said.

When Elwood didn't follow right away, she looked over Damien's shoulder.

"Elwood, all three of you. I'm ready," she said, and Damien felt his chest tighten and his heart begin to pound. Sacha was going to let them take her together.

When they got into the bedroom, Toro began to undress and then he lay down on the bed. Damien set her feet down as Elwood ran into the bathroom, probably to wash up. He would be fucking Sacha's mouth. The thought had Damien's cock hardening by the second as he set her feet down and then pulled his shirt up over his head.

Sacha reached for his jeans and undid them and pushed them down. He assisted, and she licked his nipple and tugged on it before caressing along his sides and then over his ass cheeks. He stepped from the jeans.

"Your hands feel incredible, baby," he told her, and then he pulled her up by her cheeks and head and kissed her deeply. He slowly pressed her backward, and when he sensed Toro's legs, he released her lips, turned her around, and gave her ass a nice firm smack.

"Damien." She gasped and gave him a surprised look over her shoulder.

"I own that ass, and I'm making it official in about two minutes. Get up there and take care of Toro."

She climbed up onto Toro and immediately sank down onto his cock. Toro ran his hands along her body to her back and brought her down for a deep, sensual kiss.

"Damien?" He heard his name and turned to the right to see Elwood drying off his cock with a towel and holding a tube of lube under his arm. He dropped the towel and tossed him the tube. He gave him a wink.

"Ready?" he asked.

"Toro. Oh God." Sacha moaned aloud and threw her head back.

She looked like a goddess as Damien stepped closer and caressed along her hips and to her ass. He stared at her backside.

"Oh yeah, I'm ready," Damien said, and Elwood got onto the bed.

Sacha was rocking harder, faster as she rode Toro. He was moaning and cupping her breasts, and then he glanced to the left and gave Elwood a wink.

Damien pressed kisses to her shoulder.

"I'm going to get this ass ready, baby. We're taking you together. One team, one unit."

"Oh God." She moaned, and Toro chuckled.

"She wants it bad. She's fucking coming like a faucet, Damien. Come on."

She lowered down over his chest, and Damien squeezed some lube to her ass and began to work it in there. When she shifted her ass back, thrusting up and down against his fingers and Toro's cock, he knew she was going to be able to handle the three of them together.

"Come here, woman. I've got to feel that sexy mouth of yours," Elwood told her. He caressed her shoulders and hair, bringing his cock closer to her mouth.

She opened immediately, the sight igniting something carnal and wild inside of Damien.

"Fuck, that's hot. Watching our Sacha suck Elwood's cock. Feel good, Elwood?" Toro asked him. He ran his hands through her hair and began to rock his hips.

"Feels fucking incredible."

Damien stroked his fingers a little faster into her ass. He then pulled his fingers out and added more lube. Taking a hold of his cock, he looked at Sacha's ass as he held one of her ass cheeks. He ran his cock back and forth over her puckered hole.

"Fuck, man, get in there already. She's humming and moaning against my cock, and I won't last. Fuck," Elwood complained.

"Take her, Damien. She's ours in every way," Toro told him as he gripped her hips and thrust upward.

Damien couldn't hold back.

He slowly pressed the tip of his cock to her anus. She moaned louder. He continued to stroke deeper, pressing against the tight rings and sinking all the way in until he felt a plop sensation. They all moaned aloud.

"Holy fuck," Damien said.

He gripped her hips and looked down at the sight. His cock lost between the globes of her ass, Toro sucking on her breast and tugging, Elwood with his teeth clenched as he stroked into her mouth. They were one. It was official, and nothing had felt more incredible, ever.

She pushed back against him, and he took it as a hint to begin moving. She adjusted immediately as he began nice, steady strokes in and out of her ass. Under her, Toro countered his thrusts, and she simultaneously sucked and bobbed her head against Elwood's cock.

"Holy God, this is amazing. So fucking amazing."

"How does her ass feel, Damien? How fucking good is it?" Elwood asked as he ran his palm along her ass and gave it a smack and then a squeeze.

"She's fucking tight. It feels incredible." He stroked in and out of her ass faster and faster.

"Oh hell," Elwood said and began to pump his hips as he gripped Sacha's hair.

He cried out in a deep, guttural moan as he came in her mouth. Under her, Toro followed.

"Holy fuck, baby. I love you," Toro said, and Sacha moaned as she shook and came.

"Oh God. Oh." She shivered and convulsed and Damien moved faster, trying to seek his release, shocked and touched that Toro had told her he loved her. Damien knew he loved her, too, as he stroked deeper, faster and then held her hips and came in her ass.

He tried calming his breathing, and he slowly laid kisses along her shoulder while he massaged her back and then her hips and ass, pulling slowly from her ass. His cock felt so sensitive as it slid out, the cool air colliding against the sensitive muscle.

He stepped away, and Elwood was there with a washcloth and towel.

Toro kissed her deeply then lay her on her side as he pulled from her body last.

She moaned softly, placed her arm over her head, and allowed them to take care of her and clean her up.

Damien lowered down between her legs and kissed her belly then over the bruising on her ribs. She opened her eyes, and he saw the love in them, and he knew this was perfect. She ran her fingers through his hair as he continued to kiss a path from her belly to her breasts and then to her lips.

"I love you. You're perfect, and you complete us."

A flash of fear, or maybe uncertainty, went across her eyes, and then she smiled and pulled him closer as she rose up so that their lips touched. He couldn't help but to feel as though she was avoiding saying how she felt, but he knew she felt it, too. It would take time still for Sacha to let go and open her heart completely. He realized it didn't matter. They loved her and would show her exactly how amazing this relationship would be and how making love together like this bound not only their bodies but also their hearts and souls as one. Nothing would destroy that love. Nothing.

Chapter 5

"We've got a major fucking problem," Chordero said to Striker as Axel joined Chordero in the control room.

"What?" Axel asked.

"Franco Smith has gone missing."

"Gone missing? Like what do you mean? He never came back from Iraq?" Axel asked.

"No, I mean he came back and never made it out of the airport parking lot. He arrived three nights ago and landed after eleven. His car was found with his duffel bag inside and both doors opened."

"They took him, and we're just finding out about this now? Holy fucking shit, they know Sacha has the thumb drives. They're going to use her brother to get to her and get those back," Falcon said to Chordero.

"Exactly. I think we're going to have to make a strategic move here. Riley placed those codes and the hidden password on the drives. We have that. We just need those damn drives," Chordero said. He knew it was a bad situation. Her brother could get killed. Hell, they could go after her father, too.

"But she won't give them to us if we contact her and the Vancouver brothers. We'd have to explain that Charro was working with us trying to find out who the conspirators were."

"Axel, we can't give up the existence of Strike Force 1."

"How the hell else are we going to get her to work with us, give us those thumb drives so we can decode what Riley placed on them? We also need to figure out who Black Out is and how we can take them down before they strike again. Maybe Sacha knows?" Axel asked.

Chordero ran his fingers through his hair. "This is a clusterfuck of a situation. They will all die, and innocent people will, too, if we don't find out where Black Out is going to strike again and figure out who they are and destroy them."

"I think she's earned our trust. She took out more than a dozen highly trained terrorist soldiers. I'd say she's the real fucking deal," Axel added.

"And she evaded capture and got out of the country. She's capable, and if we can ensure her brother's safe return, then we can get her cooperation," Falcon said.

"We don't even know who has her brother or where they might be," Chordero told them.

"We can figure that out. I'll hack into the security cameras at the airport and get a look at the abductors. If I can get a clear make of the get-away vehicle, I'll do my magic. You should call Maddox. Guaranteed that he'll want to be part of this. He's also close with her old man. He'll be the next one these guys might go after to get to Sacha."

"She probably doesn't even know that they have her brother," Chordero said.

"They'll find a way to make that information surface. We need those thumb drives. We need to identify the leaders of this terrorist organization and fast. If Riley was correct, they are planning something, and it's going to take place soon. I guess we have no choice. We have to find her and get to her before these assholes do."

* * * *

Sacha felt her chest tighten and that bit of anxiety hit her. She was panicking. Toro had told her he loved her. Damien and Elwood looked at her, ready to say they loved her, too, if she read their expressions correctly. It scared her. She didn't know what to do. This was happening so fast, and how could she accept it? Not now. Not when she was placing them in danger and had no idea what was happening in regards to Black Out. They needed to resolve this situation. She couldn't just forget about everything and move on with some fantasy life that Charro had in mind for all of them. Could she?

She shook the thoughts from her head as she slowly got out of bed. She eased out from Elwood's arm and slid down to the rug in order to not wake him. It was dark outside, and the blinds wide open. She shivered. Then she crossed her arms in front of her and pulled the throw blanket off the recliner. She eased it around her shoulders and then leaned against the window frame.

She felt different. She felt off kilter, and she knew exactly why. When she was under the covers, in bed with her men deep inside of her, making love to her, she was different woman. The way they made her feel, the depth of their ability to touch her in a way no other human being ever had, was magical and life altering. Last night they'd made love together. The first time the three of them were inside of her, the emotions, the power of the bond that instantly formed had practically shocked her into tears. She fought to not cry, to not let go fully out of fear of being vulnerable and weak. She had shown Damien, Toro, and Elwood such weakness in many ways, and that wasn't who she was. From the time she'd laid eyes on them as they snuck into her hellish nightmare of a situation, she'd felt the changes coming. Then to be so weak and in pain that she'd allowed Damien to bathe her then continued to let him do it for days longer than necessary just to feel his hands on her and to feel that intimate human contact was so unlike her. She was a force, an independent machine, well trained, well equipped to not need what other women, other human beings, needed. Compassion, love, affection, a simple thing like a hug.

They'd broken her down with one glance from those sexy blue eyes, one stroke of a finger under her chin, a firm hold around her waist, a glance while they worked side by side. She saw them in everything she did, she thought, she imagined. They were becoming part of her, and she couldn't fight it even if she wanted to.

But she wasn't being fair to them. She couldn't be their lover, their mate under cover and then a soldier out of bed. It felt wrong and dishonest, and one thing was certain. Marines were honest people.

She sighed as she thought about her family, her father, her brother, and all that had transpired over the years to bring her to this place and to this moment. Her focus and agenda was changing. She really didn't want to jump into the unknown anymore. She didn't want to leave them for a mission in the heat of battle and be the one they worried about not returning. She had a feeling they would never let her leave them. It made her think of Charro again. He had a plan, and it was becoming clearer. She couldn't be hundred percent certain this was his intention, but when he'd told her he wanted her to meet his family and to explore their attraction, she knew he meant to make her leave the Corps. He was done, too. Tired of it all.

It made her think of the places Charro had disappeared to, and that brought her back to the painful idea that he could have possibly been working another angle to the mission. She remembered him disappearing from time to time and that he'd used the excuse of needing alone time or time to work out and keep sharp. What had he been doing?

Her head was spinning. She needed to do something and help identify these men of Black Out. She wouldn't let anything happen to them because of her. There had to be someone they could trust to help her. But who?

She heard the movement behind her, and a moment later strong arms wrapped around her waist and a large, warm hand cupped her breast. She closed her eyes and eased back against Damien.

"Are you okay?" he whispered and kissed her neck.

She nodded. He eased his palm lower and over her belly, and she parted her thighs, needing to feel his fingers stroke her. It was so natural, so instant how she reacted and opened for him. His fingers parted her pussy lips.

"You feel warm and wet, Sacha. What are you doing over here all alone?" he asked and suckled her neck, eliciting a soft purr as he hit a sensitive spot. His fingers stroked her pussy.

She gripped the window frame and spread her legs wider. The blanket fell from her body as Damien spread her thighs with his and aligned his cock with her pussy from behind.

He slid his hand up her back, under her hair to the base of her neck, and she lowered her head submissively as he released a long sigh. She closed her eyes and absorbed the feel of him touching her, possessing her. She swallowed hard as he eased his cock into her entrance from behind then slid it back and forth over her pussy then to her anus.

"Please, Damien." She begged for it. No longer could she hold her ground and not give in. She wanted him deep inside of her, taking away the negativity, the fear and anxiety of what was to eventually come.

"I need you, too, Sacha. Every moment, as often as possible."

He eased his cock into her cunt and slid all the way in. She pushed back slowly, calmly, wanting to absorb every sensation and lock it away in her mind and in her heart for eternity.

In and out, he took his time, leisurely making love to her, stroking and caressing her body. His hands felt so amazing. They glided up her back then to her shoulders as he thrust a little harder. Then they eased down her arms to her wrists and clasped their fingers together as they lay on the window sill. He thrust deeper, still maintaining a slow pace, and she felt the difference. She gave in to his control. She trusted him and so badly just wanted to let go and give all of herself to him. His lips pressed against her shoulders and then her back as he continued a torturous slow thrust into her needy cunt.

"So beautiful. Every inch of you is perfect, baby. Every inch."

His lips pressed against her again and again. She was lost in the rhythm of his kisses, along with the stroke of his cock as he claimed her heart and soul. Again and again he continued until she was in trance, filled with love and desire.

"Damien."

"Yes, baby, do you feel it? Isn't it incredible, baby?" he asked and thrust a little faster, picking up his pace as he squeezed his fingers with hers and rocked into her.

"Yes, so good." She moaned, and he picked up the pace a little faster.

"Fuck, baby, you're so wet. Holy shit, Sacha." He thrust faster, deeper, and pulled his hands from hers, grabbed her hips, and began to thrust so hard, so fast that she cried out her release. "I love you, baby. Tell me you feel it, too. Don't hold back. Don't deny it."

He continued to thrust and command her, telling her to admit her emotions, and she felt overwhelmed with love and adoration for him and for Toro and Elwood.

Their bodies slapped together, his fingers gripping her hips so tight as he grunted and thrust.

"Say it, Sacha. Don't lie, baby. Say it." He raised his voice, and she cried out as he came inside of her.

"I love you, too. I love all three of you. I do, I do.", The tears spilled from her eyes, and her heart hammered. He wrapped his arms around her and hugged her and kissed her.

"I know you do, sweetheart. Everything is going to be just fine. I promise you."

"We promise you."

She turned to the left. Toro and Elwood were sitting on the bed, watching her and Damien.

Damien eased out of her and then turned her around and hugged her tight. He kissed her deeply and then lifted her up and carried her back to bed.

"Together. She needs us to love her together," Damien said as he lay her down on top of Elwood. She locked gazes with his blue eyes as he reached up and caressed her tears away.

"It's okay to be vulnerable when you're guarded by men you trust. Don't ever hold back, Sacha. I love you." He pulled her down for a kiss, and she kissed him right back as Toro prepared her body to make love to the three of them once again.

Chapter 6

Damien was in the computer room while Sacha and Toro were upstairs in the shower. He was typing away on the computer when Elwood walked in. He stood in the doorway, arms crossed.

"What's up?" Damien asked.

He didn't answer as Damien finished what he was doing and then rolled the chair to the side to face Elwood. He raised one of his eyebrows at his brother. Elwood was a big guy, filled with muscles, who was capable of just about anything. Seeing him with Sacha made him love his brother even more so. He trusted him and Toro with his life as well as Sacha's. He wouldn't want this relationship without them both fully on board.

"What are we going to do?"

"About what?" Damien asked.

He looked out in the hallway and then walked farther into the room.

"About Sacha. I don't want her leaving here. I don't want her going back even if this shit blows over."

He understood what his brother was saying. He felt anxiety about it, too, but this was all new to all of them.

"She won't be going anywhere for quite some time, Elwood."

"We don't know that. You called Sparrow. Any day now he's going to call with something, and I know it isn't going to be good. She'll want to finish this mission, despite the dangers. I don't think we should allow it."

"Allow it?"

"Yes, allow it. She's our woman. I'm not letting her go back into this shit. I don't know about you and Toro, but I certainly won't be able to handle her being active duty and going off on another mission like this botched one. It isn't going to happen," he said in a deep, angry voice.

"Calm down. I understand how you feel, but I think you're jumping the gun talking about it. She isn't going anywhere until these leaders of Black Out are identified and located. I was able to pull up all the information on our two senators and congressman. All three of them are up for re-election. They're in the public eye as much as possible, and you know that that means."

"Easy targets. Fuck." Elwood took a seat in the other chair.

"Show me what you have so far."

Damien's cell phone rang. It was the secure line. He put it on speaker.

"Sparrow, what's up?" he asked, recognizing the number.

"Heavy shit for you and your brothers and that sexy Marine."

"Sexy Marine?" Elwood asked, sounding pissed off.

"Hey, Elwood, didn't know you were there. Is the calmest one of you there, too?"

"You know Toro is the least calm. What's going on?" Damien asked.

"Well, I think it's safe to say that your little Marine has gotten herself in quite the situation. These men, this group of terrorists, are bad ass. Apparently they must want whatever Sacha has, badly, because her name is popping up all over the radar, good and bad."

"What the fuck do you mean?" Damien asked.

"I mean this group is after her. Maybe because she took out over a dozen of their men, but they want her. So badly that they may have just upped the ante a bit."

"How so?" Elwood asked.

"Franco is missing."

Damien leaned forward in his seat. "What?"

"Yeah, looks suspicious. Police found a car with two doors open and his duffel bag in the back seat. His keys were on the ground. The surveillance tapes of the parking lot have gone MIA, and quickly. Like before the cops could even think of grabbing them."

"Shit," Elwood replied.

"Shit is right. I've got some feelers out there but need to be careful."

"Can you find out who took him and where?"

"Working on it, brother. This is heavy shit. You'd better prepare her. I don't know what she has that they want, but it could just get Franco killed."

"What?" Sacha asked as she and Toro came into the room.

"Need to go. I'll touch base as soon as I know more."

Damien looked at Sacha.

"What's going on? Who was that? What was he saying about Franco?"

"He's missing," Damien told her.

She straightened her shoulders and stared at him. "Missing?"

"It looks suspicious. He disappeared at the airport in the parking lot. The surveillance video has been confiscated, and no one knows how it happened or who could have possibly taken him if that is the case," Elwood said to her.

"From our government. So they're onto this, too, now. They'll get him killed. I need to know who took him and where they took him. Is it to Kabul? Are they in the States? They aren't supposed to do that hit for another week."

"Sacha, we don't know. Our source who just called doesn't know either," Damien told her.

"Well, what the hell am I supposed to do? Wait here for your source to say they found Franco's body?" She raised her voice and began to pace.

"Calm down and we'll work this out."

"You don't know these men. They will kill Franco to get these thumb drives. There is more information on them. Who the hell has the password? The same fucks who set us up?" she asked, and Toro went to take her hand and pull her close to calm her, but she pulled back. "No, Toro. This is the reality of what's to come. A hug is not going to make this right. I need to focus, and hanging around here, living out some fantasy, and acting like the shit isn't about to hit the fan is not going to work anymore. I need to know where Franco is."

"You can't go out there looking for him, and even when we find him, a plan will need to be made."

"You are not my commanding officer, Damien. I don't answer to you, to anyone, especially not now when this just got a whole lot more personal."

Damien opened his mouth and stepped forward to react, but his cell phone rang again. He knew that Toro was pissed off by her reaction. Hell, he was pissed off, too, and had known she would be angry. She was right. It was getting worse.

"Hello?" He answered the phone, not bothering with speaker. Sparrow had gotten a location.

"How did you do that?" He asked Sparrow.

"Put a few things together. There were surveillance tapes along the exits by the parking pay booths. Got a fuzzy image of his van and it speeding away. Took a chance and located it."

"You think he may be there? That it could be the men who took him?"

"That's my hope. I can have some people check it out, give you some info on security and what not. It's an hour from Wellington."

"Yes."

"She's there, isn't she? Wants to head out after the men who took Franco?"

"Yes," Damien said, giving the one word answer as Sacha stared at him.

"Don't let her leave there. There are others looking for her."

"Others?"

"Yes. Give me some time."

"Got it."

He disconnected the call.

"Who was it?" she asked.

"Just an update. They're working on checking the security at the location where they think these people are holding Franco. It's an hour from here."

She stepped closer.

"Write it down."

"No," he replied.

He saw her expression change to shock as her eyes widened, and then anger as she gritted her teeth and kept her fists at her sides. She was being stubborn and emotional. He would feel the same way if one of his brothers were abducted and being used to lure him out.

"You're not going to tell me where these men, the ones I had to escape from, the ones who took my brother, are holding him? Are you fucking kidding me, Damien?" She raised her voice.

"You're not going after them and especially not gung ho and all fired up. They'll kill you, and they more than likely want these thumb drives," Toro said to her.

She looked to each of them, and he knew this was bad. She suddenly stepped back.

"What happened to the whole trust factor?"

"What is that supposed to mean, Sacha?" Elwood asked her.

"You tell me. I'm supposed to trust you? I don't even know who you're talking to. That's my brother. These men want the thumb drives I risked my life for and that Charro died trying to get."

"So you forget what we shared these last few weeks? You want to walk into what is more than likely some ambush and you think we're going to let you go with a good luck?" Elwood asked with his hands on his hips, squinting his eyes at her with an angry expression on his face.

"And some ammo since I don't have any. Or do you still think I want to hurt myself and maybe the three of you?" she asked sarcastically.

"You're not going. You're our woman, and we will protect you, not send you back into harm's way," Toro stated.

"I'm a soldier, a Marine, and this is my mission, my fight."

"You're our woman, our lover, and we're not sending you in there. We need more information."

"So what you're telling me is, because the three of you fucked me and claimed me as your woman, I'm no longer allowed to do my job and finish this mission?"

"Fucked you?" Elwood asked.

"Calm down. Everyone just calm down," Damien yelled, and they were all looking angry and pissed off. Sacha was shaking her head in disgust and biting her lip. Toro had his arms crossed and blocked the doorway in case Sacha tried to leave and Elwood gave her the once-over and ground his teeth.

"The first thing we need to do is get organized with our next steps. If Sparrow calls back and has good intel on the place, then we make a plan. A good solid plan that won't get anyone killed," Damien said to them.

"How far is the location from here? I want to know everything. I have a right to know everything, Damien, or that's it. You're whole trust thing is out the window," she said firmly. She was stubborn as damn hell but tough.

"It's an hour from here."

Her eyes widened, and she licked her lower lip. "You think they're getting close to here? You think they're smoking me out?"

"Yeah," Toro said, sounding sarcastic.

"Damn it. Give me the coordinates. Let's start getting a plan together," Elwood said and walked over toward the other computer station.

Damien looked at Sacha. "Sit here and we'll go over what Sparrow has for us thus far. We'll make a plan, and we'll try to initiate it. But we need to be smart about this."

Sacha nodded and took the seat next to him. His gut clenched with concern. He understood his brothers' fears. He had them, too. Sacha was part of them now, and they loved her, wouldn't want anything to happen to her, but these assholes were playing hardball now. She covered his forearm with her hand, and he looked at her. Even that simple touch affected him, aroused him, and made him feel protective of her.

"My father. They could go after my father next."

"I've got it covered. I'll get the message to Ivan, Sparrow's brother. He's on watch there, right?" Toro said to Damien, but his eyes were on Sacha.

"Yes. Tell him to be careful."

"Got it."

* * * *

"She is not going to come here. We're trained to die for our country," Franco said to the guard who was standing by the doorway.

Franco was now lying on his side, his lip bloody and eye bruised up from trying to escape from the vehicle. He'd gotten one of the guys but hadn't expected the other two in the darkness of the van. They'd driven for a while, and he wasn't sure how far they were from Newark, but if they'd headed north, he feared they were moving closer to Sacha's location. He wondered if these men knew where she was.

He also worried about their father. These men would do anything to get to Sacha, especially if she'd killed their men and stolen things they needed.

From what he could tell, there were only four of them, but they were heavily armed. They were in constant communication through radio with their commander or whoever was in charge of them. What struck Franco as being so odd was that these men looked like Americans but spoke with accents, as if from Pakistan. They even spoke the language. He didn't get it, but he hoped his sister didn't give in to their demands. Hopefully the Vancouver brothers were keeping her head above the water and remaining focused.

Don't come here, Sacha. Please don't fall into their trap.

* * * *

Sacha was in the armory with Toro. They were preparing the weapons and supplies to infiltrate the warehouse where the men were holding Franco. She was setting up her bag when Toro pulled her by her arm, turning her toward him.

He pointed at her.

"You're the only fucking person I have ever met that can get under my skin so easily. I can't believe what you said back there. That you think because we had sex that now we think we're in control of you. Really? I love you. You said you loved me and my brothers, too. So what the fuck gives, Sacha?" he asked her.

She stared up at him. She wasn't surprised by his reaction and the anger directed at her. She'd insulted him and the others and what they shared.

"I'm sorry, Toro. I was pissed off. You have to understand how difficult this is for me. I'm used to doing things on my own, even dangerous, life-threatening things. They abducted my brother because of me. I don't want anything to happen to you guys, too."

"We told you that we're going to help you, and that's the plan. Haven't we done so?"

"Yes, of course you have." She bent down to continue to prepare the bag. In her mind she knew what she needed to do. She needed to protect Damien, Toro, and Elwood. She couldn't get them killed because of her problems. Charro would never forgive her.

"We have a plan in motion," he said as he finished packing up the next bag.

"I know, and I don't fully agree with Damien going in first."

"Well, you don't have much of a choice," Elwood said from the doorway.

"It isn't right. I should go in first."

"And get killed?" Toro asked.

Now she was insulted. "Do I look like I just got out of boot camp?" she asked, sarcastically.

"No, baby, you look like you just walked out of *Playboy* with that body of yours."

Elwood headed straight toward her. She stood up, prepared to step back, but he was too quick. He snagged her around the waist and kissed her deeply. In no time at all, he had her pressed up against the wall and his hands were undoing the zipper on her jeans.

"How do you guys do this to me? How?" she asked, panting and helping him remove her top.

Toro placed his palm against the wall and gripped her chin, tilting it up toward him as Elwood removed her jeans, panting, then stepped from his pants.

"Because we're made for one another, baby," Toro said then kissed her. He released her lips when Elwood lifted her up and pressed her against the wall.

"I've thought about taking you here in this room, surrounded by an arsenal of weapons," he told her as he unclipped her bra and cupped her breasts. He used his hips to keep her in place and pressed against the wall. She ran her hands up his chest.

"Really? Where else have you thought about fucking me?" she asked him.

"Out in the woods, on the kitchen table."

"Over the arm of the couch in the living room," Toro added.

She felt her body hum with need. They turned her on and made her forget what was happening and how dangerous this was going to be.

"Kiss me, Elwood. Make me forget just for a little while."

He kissed her, and he stroked into her cunt at the same time. He didn't go slowly. He stroked fast and deep, taking her breath away as he pulled from her mouth and held her hips in place.

"We're part of one another, baby. Stop fighting it. We're always going to want to protect you and be by your side. Always."

His words excited her, touched her, and she wished she could give them that. Could let go and just be their woman, their lover, and live here in Wellington in a normal life and loving relationship. Could she? Could they get through this together?

He thrust his hips harder and faster against her, and she cried out as he stroked so deeply. She didn't care about anything right now but easing that deep, inner itch inside of her and being claimed by Elwood. She held on to his shoulders and counter thrusted against him until she felt herself begin to go over the edge.

"Elwood, faster, harder Elwood, please."

"Fuck, Sacha. Fuck." He grunted, and she came, gasping for air as Elwood continued to stroke deeper and deeper before he held himself still and came.

She wrapped her arms around him and hugged him to her breasts.

"I can't believe what you do to me. What the three of you do to me." She held him tightly.

"You do it to us, too, baby. That's why we're in this together. Trust us, we've got your six," Toro said, and she closed her eyes and waited for her breathing to calm as she relished the feelings that consumed her.

They would get through this. They had to because, if something happened to one of her men, life wouldn't be worth living. Her life would be over, too.

Chapter 7

"Falcon, I've got eyes on the building. We've got at least seven in total on guard. Three on the outside perimeter, and I counted four inside," Axel told Falcon.

"Prepare to move in on my signal," Falcon replied through the wrist mic.

He looked around the area. It was quiet, around three in the morning. He was about to give the signal when he saw the other movement.

"Hold up. We've got company," he said into his mic then watched as two individuals in black approached the front of the perimeter.

"Yes we do. Got two back here. What do we do?" Axel asked.

"Hold your position. Let's see who the hell this is and what they think they're going to do."

"But what if they're coming in for Franco?"

Falcon watched as the two individuals took out the first two guards and were on route to intercept the next two.

"They're doing the dirty work, and then we'll move in."

* * * *

Sacha and Toro worked side by side to sweep the front entryway of the guards. They were swift and quiet. Toro was impressed with her capabilities. He had a mix of emotions working this rescue mission with his lover. It was hard to focus on his job, his responsibilities, when she was so close to him and doing her part, too. He had to rely on her and trust her to cover him, and she had to do the same for him. But as they took out the three men and made it into the building, he couldn't help but be impressed with her.

As they rounded the corner, they heard the moaning. She stepped a little forward, and he placed his hand over her waist to pull her back behind him. He looked down at her and held her gaze with a serious expression, indicating for her to remain still, and she did. She accepted his authority and leadership.

Then they heard the whisper in their earpiece receivers from Damien.

"We've got company. Four men, watching from the wooded area. Can you two handle the other four individuals inside?"

Toro glanced at Sacha. She nodded and looked behind them then back in front of them with her gun in hand.

"Got it," Toro replied.

He looked at her as he lowered his wrist. He didn't want anything to happen to her. But then they heard the cry of pain and something fall over onto the ground. Her eyes squinted, and he saw the anger, the emotion in them. They needed to save Franco. He nodded and signaled for her to go first.

As they made their way through, they heard some commotion and voices yelling. When they came into view of the large room, there was Franco tied to a chair, bloody, beaten, and slumped over. Sacha moved like lightning once she saw the man in jeans and a dark shirt strike Franco again.

"Hey, asshole, why don't you try that with me?"

The man turned, weapon drawn, and she shot him before he could pull the trigger. Toro turned to the right as one guy shot from that direction and one shot from the left. He and Sacha were nearly back to back as they took out the other three men.

They cleared the area and focused on securing their position before Sacha ran to her brother.

"Sacha? What the hell are you doing here?"

"Rescuing you," she whispered as she placed her hand against his cheek and held his gaze. Franco looked like shit.

Toro cut the ropes off of his wrists, and Franco squinted at Toro. "Toro?"

"Hey, buddy."

Then he and Sacha froze in place as they heard the words come through their earpieces.

"We've got company, and you two aren't going to believe it. Is Franco safe?" Damien asked.

"He's safe," Toro said in his wrist mic.

"Who is out there?" Sacha asked.

"Someone who is desperate to meet you, Sacha."

Toro saw the concern in her eyes, but then her focus went back to Franco.

"Can you walk?" she asked him as she tried to help him up.

"Fuck yeah. We better get out of here. They've been talking to others, planning something big, Sacha. I think it may have to do with you and Kabul."

"We'll figure it out. Let me help you," Toro said and assisted Franco from the room and they headed outside.

* * * *

The introductions weren't immediately made, but one look at Damien and Sacha knew that they had no choice but to follow these men who apparently were waiting to meet her. She focused on Franco and his medical care at some building that looked like an empty office building but actually contained hidden offices and a clinic with medical staff. She was impressed but also on guard because she knew these were some sort of secret agents.

She stepped closer to Franco after he was cleaned up and patched up. She gently caressed his hair and the small bandage over his temple. He was all bruised up. She felt terrible because she'd caused this, and it was exactly what she hadn't wanted to happen.

"Sacha, I'm fine. I've been worse off."

She shook her head. "This was what I was afraid of. That they would come after you to get to me."

Franco took her hand and held it. He stared at her.

"You and the guys got me out of there. It worked out fine. Let's not waste time discussing the what-ifs. Do you know who these men are that were waiting on you?"

She looked behind her. They were alone, but they could see the men standing with Toro, Damien, and Elwood, talking.

"I don't know them, but I'm assuming they're some sort of operatives. They must know about Black Out and perhaps even have an idea about what they're planning."

"I think so, too."

Then they saw Damien reaching for his cell phone and answering it. He looked at the other three men and squinted as he nodded but didn't speak any long sentences. He gave yes and no answers and ended with and "I understand."

One of the big men, a soldier, approached.

"Doctors say you're good. No concussion, no broken bones, just a bit banged up. You did well, Marine."

Franco looked at him and nodded and then looked at Sacha then back at the guy.

"Who are you, and what's your interest in my sister?"

The guy looked over his shoulder at the others who now joined them. Toro and Damien took positions by Sacha. Elwood kept his arms crossed, and Sacha could tell he was concerned. Their protectiveness over her did not go unnoticed.

"My name is Franco. This is Axel and Brooks. We're part of a special enforcer team for the government. Code name Strike Force 1."

"Strike Force 1?" Franco asked, sounding as if he'd heard of them before. Sacha hadn't, and she looked at Damien. He remained straight faced.

"Our commander will meet us at a secure location closer to the city. His name is Chordero. We were sent here to locate you, Sacha. Riley was an agent working for us. Charro was assisting."

"Charro?" she asked, and she felt instantly sick. Charro was a double agent or something. She felt betrayed, and then the hand landed on her shoulder. She glanced at Toro, who didn't take his eyes off of Falcon.

"Let me explain. We had sent them in there to retrieve any information on the names. The leaders of Black Out. Our organization is pretty damn secretive, but when your team was sent in to locate and remove thumb drives copied by our agent, it was done so without our knowledge. Someone from the inside, a government official we're thinking, had been informed of your mission and wanted to beat us to the punch and get those thumb drives. Your team, Charro, Riley, were all caught in the middle. Plus, Black Out must have had connections to this individual who wanted those thumb drives. We're getting closer to figuring out who that is."

"But if you knew this, why would our team be sent in there? It was a trap. You knew that."

"We didn't know anything. This is what we figured out later. Riley was killed, taken out, his cover blown, but he got those thumb drives copied and placed into that safe. He got word to Charro. Someone on your team was working with Black Out. At first, after you showed up and took out those men before they could kill Charro, we thought you were the rogue." Axel looked her over.

Damien placed his arm around her waist and kept his hand on her hip in a possessive manner. The guy squinted and then looked at the others.

"Me? Why would you think that?"

"You killed more than sixteen men. You got out of Kabul and somehow got out of the Middle East and into the States. How the fuck did you do it?"

"She's a Marine, plus she knew those thumb drives would reveal Charro's killer and her team's killers," Franco stated.

"Charro had to have trusted you to not ask for those thumb drives and to let you hold them. So many soldiers were part of Black Out that no one expected ones planted in the streets waiting on you guys," Axel added.

"When we got to the location late because our source gave a different time of action, we found Charro, and then the rest of your team, except two of them," Falcon told her.

She felt sick to her stomach as she thought about her team and about Charro.

"Who?" Damien asked.

"Well, we thought you all died there, but then our sources located Spence and Anya."

"They're alive?" she asked, shocked as she stood straighter. She hadn't realized she was partially leaning back against Damien for support.

"Don't be happy that they're alive. They were working for Black Out."

"Jesus. What the fuck is with all the double agents and spies?" Elwood asked in frustration.

Sacha immediately felt pissed off. "We weren't made aware of any of this. It was like we were set up to take the fall to cover your covert operation."

"No. We didn't know anything about Spence and Anya working for Black Out. Our agent got in there undercover and was able to copy the thumb drives . Our hope was that the drives contained the names of those individuals involved in Black Out. We caught wind of terrorist plots and hoped the drives shed light on their intended U.S. targets. That was the entire point of the operation. But then we find out about your team, and Charro had done work for us in the past. He was a contacted and given a job that would secure those thumb drives. Except the ones you would get would only contain the next hit and not the list of individuals who are part of Black Out," Axel told her.

"What other names are on those thumb drives?"

"We don't know," Axel said.

"Bullshit you don't know. You must have a feeling, some names that you're just waiting to confirm. Because one thumb drive gave the plans of their terrorist attack straight out and the other thumb drive needed a password and it wasn't the one we were provided before taking those thumb drives," Sacha said to him.

"It doesn't matter. As soon as you get those thumb drives to us, we can put in the password and get the list. Then we can start taking these individuals out before they can succeed in killing a whole lot of innocent Americans," Falcon said to her.

"Charro died trying to get those thumb drives. My whole team, the true Americans, died trying to get those. My brother was abducted. I had to go through more than a month of hell trying to get out of the Middle East and even sustained a gunshot wound. I want to know who is on that list, and I want to be part of taking them out. And where the hell are Anya and Spence now?" she asked them.

"Learning the hard way about the consequences of treason and slowly giving up other names of individuals who aided them," Axel said, and she knew what he meant. They were being questioned, perhaps tortured for information.

"We need those thumb drives. That way we can use our resources to capture those involved and also save lives," Falcon said to her.

She looked at Franco. He nodded. Then she looked at Damien, Toro, and Elwood.

"We'll need to head back. What's the plan, and where do you want us to meet up afterward?"

* * * *

"The operation has been compromised. I want to move in on the alternate plan for tomorrow night," Mahem told Dupree.

"What in the hell are you talking about? What the fuck happened?" Dupree asked. He clenched his teeth as he held the phone close to his ear and quickly made his way down the hallway and into a private area so no one could hear him.

"The brother was rescued. A dual operation between that female Marine and a team of other men. My guys are trying to identify them and the group they work for."

"Damn it. You said you could pull this off. This hit was three years in the making. Three fucking years of establishing your organization, screwing with heads, taking out people in the way. If you fuck this up any further. I'm as good as dead. My career, my life in politics, and everything we're trying to do will be finished. You're telling me Smith's fucking daughter is responsible for all of this?"

"Yes."

Dupree ran his hand along his chin. He was panicking. They weren't going to be able to kill Campbell, Lewis, and Roland. This Marine and her friends probably knew about the explosives.

"Listen, even if they got wind of the explosion, it's still not near the location of the ones we want taken out. They'll be up to their ears in dead bodies and the media making accusations of terrorist attackers while they hunt some Middle Eastern assholes down. I'm certain one of the real terrorist groups will take responsibility. We'll be covered and you will be, too," Mahem told him.

"Not if our names are on those thumb drives."

"Yours isn't on there. Mine is. I want you to transfer that money to my account we set up. I want it done before the morning because, now, we have a new plan. One that will not only take out the competition for your election but will also complete that revenge you want over Devan Smith and his two pain-in-the-ass Marine kids. The teams helping them will die, too."

"What is your plan?"

"You'll hear about it on the news. Transfer that money."

Dupree put his cell phone away and thought about the situation. He had trusted Mayhem with so much. He wasn't sure he would pull this off. Dupree thought about Devan Smith. That fucking guy had nearly caught him all those years ago and fucked his whole career. Now, here he was, his fucking daughter in the middle of this shit and potentially capable of ruining this three-year plan. If shit went wrong, and the hit was a bust, Devan was going to die and so were his daughter and son.

* * * *

Franco watched how attentive and in tune Damien, Toro, and Elwood were with his sister. He caught the exchanged glances, the light caresses, and how protective they were of her. They had feelings for his sister. And by Sacha's acceptance of their caresses and exchanged glances, it seemed she had feelings for them, too.

She sat next to Franco in the truck as they headed out toward Wellington. Elwood sat beside her as Damien drove and Toro sat in the front passenger seat. They were all quiet.

Once they arrived at the house in Wellington, everyone ventured into the house after Damien disarmed the alarm.

"I think we should keep the perimeter alarms up and the home alarm, too," Damien said, and they all agreed.

"We need to bring the equipment into the armory. Want us to take your stuff so you and Franco can talk?" Toro asked her with his hand on her shoulder.

"I can help you," she said.

"No, talk with Franco, and we'll take care of things," Damien said and she nodded and then looked at Franco.

"Come this way," she said, and he caught how the three men looked at her with concern in their eyes before she left the room.

His body was throbbing, and he couldn't wait to hit the bed but knew it would be quite some time before that happened. They had planned on meeting Strike Force in an hour.

He looked at Sacha as she took some cold bottles of water out of the refrigerator. She passed him one as he took a seat at the large counter in the kitchen.

"How is the gunshot wound? Healing well?" he asked.

"It's fine." She took a sip from the bottle.

He looked around the place. He hadn't been here in years. He'd came over one time with Charro and a few guys. They'd done some hunting and some fishing together then caught up on some much-needed sleep.

"They took good care of you, huh?" he asked.

She avoided his eyes and looked down at her water bottle.

"Yes. It's been fine," she whispered.

"Seems more than fine. They're good men. Charro's best friends, like brothers."

"I'm so glad that you're okay. I was worried," she told him, changing the subject.

"I appreciate you figuring things out and coming in to get me. I guess we have our work cut out for us dealing with Strike Force and trying to stay abreast of the situation."

"I just want this all to be over. Whoever these men, these terrorists from Black Out are, I want them captured or dead. Enough is enough." She eased away from the counter then looked at him.

"You sure you're okay?"

"I'm good, Sacha. God, I can't believe what they said. That you killed that many men, got out of there, and survived for over a month's time. Jesus. This is a fucking mess."

"You're telling me. Charro was working for them, too. I mean, what the hell is that?" She came closer to him.

He took her hand. "You could have died out there."

"I didn't though."

"No, but you shouldn't have been in the middle of that shit. How the fuck did you wind up a special operative in the fucking Middle East? In Kabul?"

"Long story, and it wasn't supposed to be so hands-on, technically. I guess it doesn't really matter. That team no longer exists."

He held her gaze as he released her hand. "So what's with you and the three Vancouver men?"

"What do you mean?" she asked, pressing a strand of loose hair behind her ear and avoiding his gaze once again.

"They care about you."

"I care about them. They're good men, and they've risked a lot to help me."

He snorted. "They're in love with you."

She looked at him and held a straight, non-emotional expression. He didn't have to wonder how she did that. Dad had taught them so well.

"It's okay to like them, to want to get involved with them, Sacha."

"Franco, please. This isn't the—"

She started to turn to walk away from him, but he grabbed her hand and held her there.

"No, Sacha, don't make the same mistake Dad did. The same mistake I made with Liz."

She squinted at him as if not understanding what he meant. "What are you saying?"

"I'm talking about Dad with Mom. Always thinking that he could never fully love her because it would hurt her too badly if he died in combat. We were taught to hold back our emotions and never fully give all of ourselves to someone. It isn't right. I fucking did it with Liz, and I lost her to a man who could give her full attention, love her completely."

She stared at him, and he saw the flash of realization in her eyes.

"You love them, too, don't you?" he asked.

"I do, Franco, but I'm a Marine first, and this mission isn't complete. Not until these terrorist assholes are behind bars or dead."

"And if these thumb drives don't reveal their identities, and if you don't catch them, then what? Are you going to chase after them, leave these guys behind, and lose the chance to be happy, in love, and safe?"

She took a few unsteady breaths. "Like you said. We're trained to not give up our full emotions and let go. I'll do what needs to be done. But I've already decided that it ends here. It ends with bringing justice to Charro and the others. We stop this terrorist act from occurring, and Strike Force can handle the rest."

He gave her a nod and looked around the place.

"I always liked visiting here with Charro and the guys. It was a safe haven, a resort for us military guys. The hunting, the fishing, the catching up with sleep for days." He smiled. "You're going to love it here," he whispered and gave her a wink.

Her cheeks turned a nice shade of red. "Don't go jumping the gun, Franco. They haven't asked me to."

"Asked you to do what?" Damien asked, entering the room along with Elwood and Toro.

"Nothing," Sacha said and walked back around the counter.

Toro was pulling water bottles from the refrigerator.

"To move in with you guys," Franco said.

"Franco," she stated firmly, and Toro wrapped his arms around her waist from behind and hugged her.

"You told him about us?" he asked.

"I figured it out." Franco looked at them as they gathered around his sister.

"And?" Damien asked, looking for a reaction, an opinion on it.

Franco smirked. "Crazy fucking Charro. He knew exactly what he was doing." He took a slug from his water bottle.

"What?" Sacha asked.

"He wanted this. He hoped for this, for his brothers and for him to settle down and be like their friends. To have a woman to love and share and provide for. He talked about it, and the next thing I know he's with you on that mission and you two are working together and getting to be such good friends. I knew he trusted them with his life and obviously with yours. So when the shit hit the fan and you called needing help, I knew exactly who would be the right ones for the job."

"Son of a bitch," Toro said, and they all chuckled.

"Charro," Elwood whispered, and they were all silent.

"So, how fucking pissed off will the old man be about this?" Toro asked him.

Franco chuckled. "Beats the shit out of me. But good luck with that. Even know she's a Marine, she's still daddy's little girl."

They chuckled, and Toro turned her around and kissed her. As he released her, smiling, Damien's cell phone rang.

"We'll be there in thirty." He disconnected the call.

"We got the meet-up spot. Let's grab the thumb drives and some more guns and ammo. It's time to end this shit once and for all."

Chapter 8

"Are you fucking kidding me? They're Americans," Chordero said as they viewed all the information Riley had encoded in the thumb drives. They had a list of all those belonging to Black Out.

"Holy shit. This was all a fucking scam to throw us all off and make us believe they were Middle Eastern terrorists. The other hits in Kabul and Iraq were all setups for this big hit. We've been thinking they were from the Middle East, but really they're rogue military from the states," Falcon said.

"Holy shit," Franco added as they started going through each individual and their history.

Mahem, Dawsen, Valen and Hazeil were all American soldiers turned rogue agents and terrorist operatives.

"Jesus, Riley and Charro uncovered everything. They busted this case wide open. We need to get information out on these men. They have to be here in the United States and ready to strike," Chordero said and started giving out orders.

Sacha was listening to everything and going through more of the material on the thumb drive.

"What about these coordinates and phone calls? Who is this person that initiated this hit on the two senators and the congressman?" Sacha asked as she looked through the printed documents next.

"I've got something here. Looks like our four rogues arrived yesterday, and some kind of money transfer went through to an account hours ago. It was sent from Senator Dupree's home computer.

"Senator Dupree?" Sacha looked at Franco.

"Could this be a political move to ensure that Campbell, Lewis, and Roland do not get re-elected?" Franco asked.

"It could very well be. Chris, can you go through all this information? We're going to need all this after we stop these men from trying to kill two U.S. senators and a congressman," Chordero said to one of the other agents helping.

"We have a location and a plan in action here. Looks like they plan to hit them at this campaign event in a week," Axel said to them.

"I don't think so. Not with us getting this close and having these thumb drives. They know that we know what the plan is. They had to be aware of Riley adding their names and all this shit to the thumb drives. They'll move up the date of this hit," Damien said to them.

"Where else are these four people supposed to be together? Can we get some sort of schedule of activities? It's obvious that they travel in groups. Look at all these events the congressman and senator have planned. They're easy targets like this." Sacha said, pointing at the sheets of paper with schedules of appearances on them.

"I got it. Oh shit," Toro said as he looked at the information.

'Today. In less than two hours, they're supposed to be at the stadium for a concert and fundraising event."

"Let's move on this fast. This will be the only opportunity we may have. Chris, you take a team and intercept Dupree at his house. I want him arrested and brought in for our personal interrogation."

"Yes, sir," Chris said and organized a team.

"Okay, let's call everyone in and get some people to that stadium. Thanks to Charro and Riley, we have the blueprints of the place and the points of interest that the bombs have been planted. We need a special team to go in and disarm Falcon," Chordero said to hm.

"I'll grab the team with Axel. We'll disarm that bomb."

"We'll provide support to take out any shooters," Damien said.

"Okay, let's do this," Chordero said. The men started to leave the room, and Sacha looked at Franco.

"I'll stay here and keep in touch with you through it all." She gave him a hug. "This ends today, Franco."

He nodded at her. As Sacha headed out of the room, Damien grabbed her hand and pulled her into another room.

He pressed her up against the wall. "I don't want you near the bomb location. I don't want you going in there."

"What? How can you ask me not to?" she asked, feeling her anger begin to boil. She started to argue, and he pressed a finger over her lips.

"It's fucking killing us to see you in this danger and to know how intense this asshole is and how badly he wants you dead. But we understand your position. We love you and want you safe, Sacha. When this is over, we're going to have to have a serious discussion about your career and the choices you make in missions."

Before she could reply, he kissed her deeply. She wrapped her arms around his shoulders and hugged him tightly. Someone knocked on the door, and they pulled apart.

"Be careful."

"You, too, Damien."

When they opened the door, Toro and Elwood appeared. They kissed her, too, and then they headed out of the building and toward the SUV.

* * * *

Mahem had everything in place. He was in position, and so were his men. This had been easy. A piece of cake. He sat in the seats at the stadium with a clear view of the three people who were going to die today. It was the perfect plan. They would set off the one explosion in the left side of the stadium, and everyone would run to the right side to escape through the exit doors. But as the senators and congressman were escorted out by security, the second explosion would occur while the snipers took their shots. There would be so much debris and fire that no one would know they'd been shot at first. It was the perfect plan.

As he looked at his watch, he waited for three more minutes. His heart was pumping fast, and a smirk formed on his face. He was three million dollars richer, the money safe in the account, and he was all set to leave the country within the hour.

He spoke into his wrist mic. "All set on snipers and detonation?"

"Yes."

He heard the response and didn't recognize the voice. "Dawson?"

As he said the name, Mahem caught sight of a group of men making their way toward the senators and congressman. They were showing ID, and that was when he spotted Sacha.

"Hit it now. Hit it now," he said into the mic.

He stood up and prepared to leave. Nothing happened. No explosion went off.

He looked ahead and saw the group of men. Military, two who called him by his name.

"Stop right there, Mahem. It's over," he yelled to him.

Mahem ran down the stairs and headed toward the open field. To the right he could see the government agents ushering out the congressman and two senators. He didn't have a clear shot. He pulled out his gun as he scaled the fence. He started to run, heard the gunfire, turned a few feet from the fence, and saw her. She leaped over the fence, flew through the air, and tackled him to the ground.

She surprised him, and he retaliated, striking her hard. They exchanged blows, and she struck him back. The bitch was strong and determined. He used his weight, and they began rolling around on the stage floor. The sound of chairs knocking over and the blows against his side from rolling into them had him gasping for breath. She was struggling for control too and countering his every move. She slammed his head, stunning him. She was relentless and just kept fighting. She wasn't going to win. He was in control here. He had to get his gun in position. A bullet would stop the bitch. She decked him again, right in the nose, shocking him. Her teeth were clenched as she fought for control of the gun, and he knew he was running out of time. He gripped it tight, felt the trigger, and pulled blindly. He pulled the trigger again, twice more, and then he felt the shots. His eyes widened in disbelief. She pulled hers, and his gut burned. She maneuvered over him, knocked the gun from his hand, and held her gun to his head as numerous men surrounded them.

"It's over, asshole. It's over."

* * * *

"What in God's name did you think you were doing? I told you to take position on the other side, away from the explosives," Damien reprimanded her as he ran his hands along her body, rechecking her.

Toro and Elwood did the same, and they all looked so wild, so freaked out.

"I was over here securing the senators and the congressman when I caught sight of Mahem sitting in the stands. He ran, and the others were too far to catch him," she told them.

"You jumped a fucking fence and dove on him," Elwood said to her.

"He fired his gun and could have killed you," Toro added.

"Well, in my family, we don't worry about the what-ifs and the could have-should have. We celebrate a win and that everyone is safe and sound."

"God damn, woman. When we get you back to Wellington…" Elwood reprimanded.

"Whoa, remember that I'm on the mic here. Sacha, we have a situation," Franco said, and they held their fingers against their receivers by their ears so they could hear him.

"Dupree is missing. Disappeared. Chris and the team found a lot of evidence at his home. They're tracking his vehicle now."

"Where is he headed, Franco?" Damien asked. They all started to walk out of the stadium and up past the seating to head to the parking lot.

"We don't know. I'll have confirmation soon."

* * * *

The moment they got into the back of the SUV, Toro pulled Sacha onto his lap and kissed her deeply. He ran his hands along her body to ensure she was indeed safe and unscathed. She kissed him back as Elwood undid her vest and then ran his hands up her shirt to her breasts.

When he released her lips, they were panting.

"I—" She started to speak, and he stopped her, reminding her about the ear- and mouthpiece and how her brother could hear them.

He was frantic with need to be close to her, to make love to her, and he knew it would be hours until they could finally all be together.

She eased up, and Elwood pulled her into his arms next and kissed her. She kissed him back and then hugged him as Damien drove the SUV out of the parking lot and out of there. Toro glanced back at her from the passenger seat. Their jobs were done. Now all they needed to do was wait to hear that Dupree was caught.

* * * *

Franco was frantic as Chris called him into Dupree's office. The rest of the team was there, searching through the home.

"He knows your father, Franco. He's been drinking, and a gun is missing from the case he left out and there's a box of bullets on the floor." Chris told him as he opened up files and showed Franco pictures of him, of their father, and Sacha.

"What the hell do you mean he knows my father?" Franco asked as he looked through the material. He didn't know about any of this.

About some sort of mission years ago when his dad had been a young Marine. He'd accused Dupree of treason and smuggling and selling U.S. weapons to African guerilla fighters to kill innocent people in villages. It was all there in the documents, along with how someone else had been held responsible.

"Jesus, this guy is bad news. Does your father still live at this address?" he asked him.

"Yes. Shit, do you think he went there to kill him?"

Chris swallowed hard..

"Let's go. It's twenty minutes from here. In the car, call your dad and warn him."

* * * *

Devan Smith was sitting in his living room watching TV. He was waiting to hear from Franco or even Sacha. Something was going down. Franco had gone missing, and he just knew that it had something to do with Sacha and her mission. He didn't dare try to contact anyone, but he'd heard from Sparrow that some shit was going down, that his kids were safe, and they would call him as soon as it was all clear.

He had paced the porch for a while then headed inside. The sound of his cell phone ringing made him reach for his hip, and he realized he'd left the phone on the kitchen table. He got up and headed that way, and as he did, he saw Bobby Dupree standing there, pointing a gun at him.

He looked like hell.

"What's going on, Dupree?" he asked calmly, despite the fact that he could tell the man was fucked up. He looked a mess with red-rimmed eyes, his shirt undone. He was white as a ghost, and his hands shook. He looked unstable, and Devan wondered what in God's name was going on.

"You and your fucking shit-ass kids ruined everything. Everything."

Devan felt his anger immediately rise. So this asshole had something to do with Sacha nearly getting killed and Franco disappearing?

"What are you talking about? What the hell are you doing here, pointing a gun at me?"

"Because you should have died years ago. I should have hunted you down in Africa and killed you then. You caused me shit there, and now your kids fucked up a three-year plan."

"I don't know what you're rambling on about. I don't know why you'd hold a grudge after all these years. You got away with murder, with selling guns to those killers."

"They were men working to make a better place for the locals."

"They were killers, eager to hunt innocent prey and get money, drugs, and power from some self-centered senator from the United States. What did you get involved in now to get so many American soldiers killed?" he asked and eased toward the right. If he could get to the door and shove through, he might have a chance of running out then reaching for his ankle gun.

"Your daughter, the bitch, killed a lot of men."

"All bad guys I'm sure."

"Men who worked for me and the team I created to secure this country's freedoms."

"Don't you mean to secure your election?" Franco said, joining them.

Devan was shocked, and so was Dupree as he turned the gun on Franco. He fired his gun and Franco ducked and weaved. It gave Devan the opportunity to grab his ankle gun and fire back. He hit Dupree in the chest, and Dupree went down. The gun fell from his hand, and Franco grabbed it.

"All clear," he yelled out, and a group of other men, agents, entered the scene.

Franco went to his dad.

"Good timing, son."

"You had it covered, but it was taking too long. Sacha wanted to wrap things up." He smirked.

He hugged his son. "Jesus. What the hell did they do to you?"

"I'm fine, Dad. Sacha and her men rescued me."

He pulled back and squinted at his son. "Sacha and her men?"

"Long story, but I don't think she'll be living around here anymore."

He looked at Franco sideways.

"There's no way the Vancouver men are going to let her out of their sights."

"All three of them?" he asked, feeling shocked but not completely surprised. He knew of a lot of such relationships. He just wanted his daughter happy and safe.

"Yup, so prepare yourself."

Devan didn't think he was quite ready for that, but all he cared about was seeing Sacha and holding her in his arms and knowing she was safe and alive. He got that wish twenty minutes later as she ran into the house, her three big military men in tow and a smile that told him she was more than okay. She hugged him tightly, and he spun her around then set her down.

"My God, baby girl. You scared me." He cupped her cheeks, and tears filled her eyes.

"Didn't you think I would make it out alive?" she asked.

"I hoped so."

"Come on, Dad, you taught me so much. I couldn't fail you and Franco." He smiled. "Never. You're one tough Marine, but remember, you're my baby girl, too."

She hugged him again, and he looked at Damien, Toro, and Elwood. He swallowed hard and gave each of them a firm expression. Sacha pulled back. She looked at them and then her dad.

"Dad, you remember Damien, Toro, and Elwood Vancouver?"

"Of course. Thank you for keeping her safe." He shook each of their hands. Franco hugged her, and they smiled at the Vancouver men.

"So, would someone like to explain exactly what the hell went down here tonight?" he asked.

"It's a long story, Dad. Got any beer?" Franco asked, and they chuckled.

He looked at the three men and then at Sacha as she went to stand with them.

"Something tells me I'm going to need a few in me as you explain what else is going on in your life, little lady, and exactly what you Vancouver brothers have in mind for my daughter."

"Dad," she scolded, and her cheeks turned a nice shade of red.

"Well, sir, we love her. We don't want her going on any more of these dangerous missions, and we intend to spend the next several weeks convincing her to move in with us, be our woman, and maybe even start a family," Damien told him, and Devan was shocked. But not as shocked as Sacha, who turned a nice shade of red and looked incredible happy and totally in love.

"You guys are going to need some heavy artillery and major backup. Let's talk," he said, and they all laughed.

Sacha stood there wide eyed, and they headed into the living room while the agents and police took care of getting Dupree to the emergency room. They would then question him and hopefully charge him with so many things he wouldn't ever see anything but bars around him for the rest of his life.

Epilogue

They hadn't even made it through the garage and up the stairs before Elwood began to remove Sacha's clothing. They were all stripping and tossing underwear, her bra, and shoes as she backed up and Elwood pressed her against the hallway wall. He covered her mouth and kissed her then lifted her up and carried her down the hallway. She ran her fingers through his hair, and he felt the tingling sensations travel under his skin. He fell to the bed with her underneath him as he continued to feast on her. She wrapped her legs around him and thrust against his very hard cock. As Elwood eased from her lips, he stared down into her eyes.

"I need you so badly. I thought we would never make it home."

"So do we," Toro said as he lay on the bed naked, his legs hanging off the edge.

"I've got the lube," Damien said, naked and tapping the tube against his palm.

Elwood cupped her breasts, squeezing them, tugging on them as he rose up and stood.

"Come here, baby. Now," Toro ordered, and she immediately rolled over and then straddled his hips.

She sank down on Toro, and they both moaned.

"Sweet mother, I missed you. Fuck, baby, I won't last. This is going to be a quick one."

She began to ride Toro, thrusting up and down on his lap and moaning as she gripped his shoulders and pressed her ass back.

"Here," Damien said to Elwood, handing him the lube as he climbed up on the bed and gently took Sacha's face between his hands and kissed her.

She reached for his cock and stroked him until it was too much. He pulled from her lips and then he fed her his cock. Sacha sucked Damien's dick into her mouth, and Damien caressed her hair, staring at her with love and passion in his eyes, and Elwood felt his chest tighten with love for her.

He eased some lube into her tight ass and worked his fingers in there. As he pumped and rotated, she shifted back, and he knew she wanted his cock in there now. He made sure she was well lubricated as she rode Toro and sucked on Damien's cock, waiting for him to join them.

"You're all ours, Sacha. We're going to spend every hour, every day, loving you and loving this sexy body."

He eased his fingers out and then replaced them with his cock. As he slid slowly into her ass, he felt his entire body shiver with desire and love for her and for his brothers. There was nothing in this world like making love to Sacha together. It bound them all, hearts and souls, and made a love that could survive anything. He started to move, felt the plop as he sank his cock all the way in, balls deep. That was it. The fears he had all this time came to surface. The worry that she could have died, the sight of her leaping the fence and tackling Mahem, a terrorist killer, was all too much to recall as he fucked her faster. Harder, deeper, he sank in and out of her, trying to absorb the fact that she was indeed safe, that she had survived, and that she was his and his brothers' woman to protect and love forever.

"I love you, baby," he said to her as he began a relentless fast pace, along with his brothers as they made love to her.

Damien came first and then eased out of her mouth and kissed her cheeks and head. Toro followed, and Elwood came last. They remained close to her, kissing her, loving her, and relishing the aftermath of their lovemaking until they did it all over again. It was a hell of a night and would be a hell of a life with Sacha.

* * * *

"So what do you think?" Damien asked Sacha as they walked into Crossroads and took a seat at the bar. Outside the snow was falling, and it added to the Adirondack feel of the place and this beautiful town called Wellington.

"I love it. There are so many people here, and they know you guys, too."

Toro pressed up against her back and kissed her neck. "They're friends of ours. For the most part these are locals," he told her.

"Hey, to what do we owe this pleasure of seeing the Vancouver brothers out and about?" one man asked as he joined them with a woman and a few other men.

"Chief Cummings we'd like you to meet Sacha."

The chief widened his eyes, and the woman next to him smiled.

"Seriously? Oh my God, where have you been hiding her? She's gorgeous," the woman said and then came closer and reached out her hand. "I'm Bethany, and these men are Chancellor and Collin, the chief's brothers."

"And this is our woman," Collin said as he wrapped an arm around Bethany's waist and kissed her shoulder. She laughed, and the guys all shook hands and then the brothers shook her hand in greeting.

"It's so nice to meet you," Sacha said to them, and soon other people came over. They were buying them drinks, and Sacha was meeting all their friends and their friends' women. It looked as though Wellington had a lot of ménage relationships.

"So what do you do, Sacha?" Chief Cummings asked.

"She's a Marine." Elwood told him.

The men widened their eyes and looked her over.

"Nice. Should have figured it would take a Marine to settle you three down," Collin said to them.

"Who said we were settled down?" Elwood asked.

Everyone chuckled.

"In that case, you're still available if we need you for tracking and some special missions in Wellington and the surrounding areas?" Riley asked as he took a slug from his beer.

"Hell yeah, and since we've been trying to talk Sacha into retiring from the Corps and working with us, you can add another valuable tracker and hunter to your list."

"Damn, you lucky bastards," the bartender said from behind the bar, and they all laughed.

Sacha leaned back against Damien as their friends joined them and talked about the upcoming holidays, the tourists, and hikers that often got lost and needed rescuing, and all the fun things that Wellington had to offer. She couldn't help but to smile and wonder if she really could retire from the Corps and live a normal life with her three Marines. Was she really ready for that?

"Hey, I love you, no matter what you decide in a few weeks. We'll always be here for you, Sacha. Believe me, Wellington is not a boring place to live. There's always an adventure or two popping up and the need for good soldiers, well trained and able to do more than typical civilians." Damien told her.

Riley's cell phone went off, and he answered it and then cursed.

"Hey, guys. We got two hikers, boyfriend and girlfriend, who have been lost for several hours. Last word was that they were somewhere maybe between Spook Rock and Devil's Peak. Up for helping us out?"

Toro looked at Sacha. "What do ya say, beautiful?"

She smiled wide. "I'm in if you have the gear."

Toro and Elwood smiled.

As the men got the details, Sacha took in her surroundings and watched as everyone volunteered to do their part in helping. Two other men Doc and Stitch, Damien had mentioned as they arrived started making thermoses of hot coffee and some food, and others organized radio contact. She and her men headed out to the SUV.

If she was going to retire and try to live a normal life with her three Marines, this place seemed absolutely perfect. She wouldn't have a worry about putting them in danger for a mission gone wrong. She wouldn't have to remain their lover under cover, and hide her true feelings and the love she really had for them. She could finally be free, have friends, enjoy the simple things, and maybe even add some more pictures to that wall in their house filled with fond memories of friends, family, and what was yet to come.

As they got into the SUV and they explained their plan of action, she felt encouraged and part of something special. They would find the lost hikers. They would help this community, and it would be a beginning of her new life in Wellington, where anything was possible. She smiled wide.

"What's that grin about?" Toro asked her.

"Just thinking how right Charro was. I'll never forget him," she said.

"None of us will, ever," Elwood told her as he took her hand, kissed the top, and smiled.

THE END

WWW.DIXIELYNNDWYER.COM

ABOUT THE AUTHOR

People seem to be more interested in my name than where I get my ideas for my stories from. So I might as well share the story behind my name with all my readers.

My momma was born and raised in New Orleans. At the age of twenty, she met and fell in love with an Irishman named Patrick Riley Dwyer. Needless to say, the family was a bit taken aback by this as they hoped she would marry a family friend. It was a modern day arranged marriage kind of thing and my momma downright refused.

Being that my momma's families were descendants of the original English speaking Southerners, they wanted the family blood line to stay pure. They were wealthy and my father's family was poor.

Despite attempts by my grandpapa to make Patrick leave and destroy the love between them, my parents married. They recently celebrated their sixtieth wedding anniversary.

I am one of six children born to Patrick and Lynn Dwyer. I am a combination of both Irish and a true Southern belle. With a name like Dixie Lynn Dwyer it's no wonder why people are curious about my name.

Just as my parents had a love story of their own, I grew up intrigued by the lifestyles of others. My imagination as well as my need to stray from the straight and narrow made me into the woman I am today.

Enjoy *Crossroads 6: Love Undercover* and allow your imagination to soar freely.

For all titles by Dixie Lynn Dwyer, please visit
www.bookstrand.com/dixie-lynn-dwyer

Siren Publishing, Inc.
www.SirenPublishing.com